I0616772

TO-MORROW?

VICTORIA CROSS

1st WORLD
LIBRARY
Literary Society

To-morrow?

Victoria Cross

© 1st World Library – Literary Society, 2006
PO Box 2211
Fairfield, IA 52556
www.1stworldlibrary.org
First Edition

LCCN: 2006930805

Softcover ISBN: 1-4218-2206-7
Hardcover ISBN: 1-4218-2106-0
eBook ISBN: 1-4218-2306-3

Purchase *"To-morrow?"*
as a traditional bound book at:
www.1stWorldLibrary.org/purchase.asp?ISBN=1-4218-2206-7

1st World Library Literary Society is a nonprofit
organization dedicated to promoting literacy by:

- Creating a free internet library accessible from any computer worldwide.
- Hosting writing competitions and offering book publishing scholarships.

To-morrow?
contributed by Tim, Ed & Rodney
in support of
1st World Library Literary Society

"Cras te victurum, cras dicis Postume semper

Dic mihi cras istud, Postume quando venit?

Quam longe cras istud, ubi est? aut unde petendum?

Cras istud quanti dic mihi, possit emi?

Cras vives? hodie jam vivere, Postume, serum est

Ille sapit, quisquis Postume, vixit heri."

MART. v. lviii.

CHAPTER I

"REJECTED! rejected!"

I crushed the letter spasmodically in my hand as I walked mechanically up and down the length of the dining-room, a rage of anger filling my brain and the blood thundering in my ears.

"Rejected! and that not for the first time. Another year and a half's work flung away - simply flung away, and I am no nearer recognition than ever. Incredible it seems that they won't accept that."

I stopped under the gasalier and glanced again through the letter I had just received.

"DEAR SIR, - With reference to your last MS., we regret to say we cannot undertake its publication, owing to the open way in which you express your unusual religious views and your contempt for existing institutions.

"At the same time, our reader expresses his admiration for your style, and his regret that your unmistakably brilliant genius should be directed towards unsatisfactory subjects. - We are," etc., etc.

The blood flowed hotly over my face, and my teeth closed hard upon my lip.

Always the same thing! rejection from every quarter.

The last clause in the letter, which might have brought some momentary gratification to a man less certain, less absolutely sure of his own powers than I was, could bring none to me.

It only served to make sharper the edge of my keen disappointment. Brilliant genius! I read the words with the shadow of a satirical smile.

What need to tell me that I possessed a power that inflamed every vein, that heated all the blood in my system, that filled, till they seemed buoyant, every cell of my brain? As much need as to tell the expectant mother she has a life within her own.

I was tired of praise, tired of being called gifted, tired of hearing reiterated by others that which I knew so well myself.

We are invariably little grateful for anything freely and constantly offered to us, and I cared now simply nothing for compliments, praise, or felicitation.

These had been given to me from my childhood upwards, and yet here, at six and twenty, I was still unknown, unrecognized, obscure, and not a single line of my writing had met the public eye.

I craved and thirsted after success far more than a fever-stricken man in the desert can crave after water, for the longings and desires of the body are finite, and when a fixed pitch in them has been surpassed, death grants us a merciful cessation of all desire, but the longings of the mind are infinite, absolutely without limit and without period; and where a physical desire, ungratified, must eventually destroy itself as it wears away the matter that has given it birth, a mental desire does not wane with the flesh it wastes, but remains ravening to the last, and reigns supreme over the death agony, up to the final moment of actual dissolution.

I had done what I could to attain my own wishes; I was not one of those idle, clever fellows who imagine talent independent of work, and who are too lazy to throw into words and commit to paper the brilliant but vague, unformed inspirations that visit them between the circling rings of smoke from their cigar.

I had no thought, no expectation, no wish even to be offered that celebrated sweet condition of the palm without the dust of the struggle in the arena.

But for me it had been dust, dust, and nothing but dust, and there were times when it seemed to blind, choke, overpower me.

My capacity for work was unlimited; labour was comparatively no labour to me. The mechanical work of embodying an idea in a manuscript was as nothing to me.

To write came to me as naturally as to speak.

Therefore work had not been wanting. Manuscript after manuscript had been completed, submitted to various publishers, and returned with thanks, with commendation, and regrets that I had not written something totally different.

And there they all stood in a pile, an irritating, distracting pile, a monument of unrequited labour, an unrealised capital, a silent testimony to the exceeding narrowness of the limits of British indulgence to talent.

My persistent ill-luck was all the more aggravating as I was not handicapped by poverty, as so many authors are. The question of terms had not been one to present a difficulty.

I had no need to ask a publisher to accept my MSS. at his own financial risk.

I was not the traditional struggling young writer of the lady novelist who treats poverty and genius as convertible terms, making up with the former quality whatever her hero lacks of the other.

No; although the combination may be very romantic, I confess, notwithstanding that I was an unrecognised author, I was not living in a garret, nor writing my MSS. by the proverbially flaring candle, nor going without my dinner in order to pay for foolscap.

But my feelings were as bitter, and the sense of disappointment as sharp, as any attic-dwelling genius' could have been, even if we suppose the lady novelist to have thrown in a conventionally consumptive wife.

In fact they were stronger because more absolute, more concentrated in themselves.

There were no pangs of hunger to distract my attention, no traditionally patient wife to look sadly at me, no responsibilities for others lying upon me and my rejected MSS.

Simply all my own desires for myself centred in them.

There was one side issue which at times seemed to include everything, to be everything in itself, but the moments when this forced itself in overwhelming prominence upon my brain were few.

The wish that I had to publish my works could not be traced to distinct motives; it did not spring from a desire to gain money, nor yet celebrity.

I was not particularly keen on fame while I lived, and I certainly had no sentimental ideas of my name surviving me.

I cared little in fact whether my name ever reached the public, provided only my works were known and read. The wish to give them out was not a thing of motive, nor thought, nor will.

It was the fierce, instinctive impulse that accompanies all creative power, the tremendous impetus towards production that is an integral part of all conceptive capacity. The same driving necessity that compels a writer in the middle of the night to rise and take his pen and commit to paper some thought or thoughts that are racing about in his brain, trying to find an outlet, that compels him to produce them as far as he is able, this same urgent impulse forces him to complete his manuscript, and when completed, to strain his utmost to give it actual life in the thoughts and brains of the public.

The pressing want to produce is as wholly natural, as innate, as independent of the individual's volition as the conceptive impulse itself.

And it was thus with me.

I could not be said to wish to publish from this or that motive, because of this, that, or the other. I was simply dominated by the instinct to do so, which grew more and more urgent as it found no gratification.

It had risen now rampant at this last rebuff, and it seemed to rage about in my brain like a Bengal tiger in a net.

I walked up and down the long dining-room, backwards and forwards, from the grate where the fire blazed to the glass-panelled sideboard at the other end, where its reflection sparkled, yawning every now and then from sheer nervous irritation. "Cursed, infernal nuisance!"

I had just muttered this when the door was pushed open, but the enterer, on hearing my exclamation, promptly drew it to again, and would have shut it, but that I caught the handle.

It was the butler.

"What do you want, Simmonds," I said.

"Nothing, sir. I was told to enquire if you was in."

"Well, I am."

"Yes, sir. Please, Mr. Hilton said was you ready for dinner?"

"Certainly; and, Simmonds, where's Nous?"

"Tied up, sir, in the stable."

"Tied up! Again! I gave orders he was never to be tied up!"

"Yes, sir; but please, sir, he was that dirty and muddy to go scrimmaging over the house, and it's the ruination of the furniture -"

"The dog is not to be tied up," I interrupted.

"Have him let loose at once, and in future remember, if he comes in wet and muddy, and chooses to lie on the drawing-room couch, let him."

The man disappeared, and I walked over to the hearth.

A minute or two later there was a scratching and whining outside the door, and I went to it and let Nous in.

He bounded over me, licked my face furiously, and scratched enthusiastically at my shirt front.

He was wet, and his fur laden with mud, as the butler had said, and my clothes suffered from his demonstrativeness, but his feelings were of more import than a dress-coat, and I would not have hurt them by checking his greeting.

"Dear old boy," I said, taking the collar off with which he had been chained up, - and just then my father came into the room.

"Ah, got back, Victor?"

"Yes," I said, looking up.

"They've rejected your last, eh?" he said at once.

"Yes. Why? Have they sent it? How did you know it was rejected?"

"By your face, my dear boy," answered my father.

"It's odd that these failures knock you up still. You must be accustomed to them now!"

That was cutting, and it cut.

"One does not easily get accustomed to anything that is against natural law," I said, coldly.

"Oh! and you mean that it is against the natural law of things that so brilliant a genius as yourself should be perpetually rejected?"

I nodded. "Just so," I answered.

"It is a pity they will not take your estimation of your own powers!"

"There is very little difference in the estimation," I said. "The difference is in the courage. I have the courage to write things they have not the courage to print. There is no question as to my powers. No one, except yourself, perhaps, has ever denied those."

"Well, why the dickens don't you write something that they will accept? Why not make up something quite conventional?"

I looked across the hearth at him with a half amused, half ironical smile, and said nothing. It is so hard to explain to an outsider the involuntariness of all real talent.

This great leading characteristic is invariably but imperfectly grasped by others.

They cannot realise it.

I was too flat in spirits and too tired in body to feel inclined to enter then into an abstruse discussion with him, and I would have let the matter slide.

His last remark to the ear of anyone who has genuine talent, whether artist or author or poet, or what you please, sounds like a sacrilegious blasphemy.

"Make up something!"

Great heavens! What an expression!

Is a writer, then, a cook, preparing a new dish? Is he a nursery maid soothing a refractory child? Is he a woman's dressmaker taking her mistress's orders?

Dinner was served just then, and we took our seats at the table in silence.

I thought I should have no need to answer.

However, when the butler had deposited the soup and shut the door after him, my father returned to the attack.

"Yes, Victor," he said in a friendly way, as if a happy solution of my difficulties had just occurred to him, "why don't you make up something quite orthodox and keep your own opinions out of it?"

I sighed and took half a glass of claret to fortify me. I saw I was in for propounding my views upon genius, and I did not feel up to it.

I could have avoided the argument, doubtless, by seeming to assent, by promising to "make up something," and saved myself a number of words.

But there is a strong impulse in me to revolt against allowing myself to seem to accept a false statement or opinion that I do not really hold.

And I pulled myself together with an effort.

"I don't think you understand in the least my view of a writer and his writings," I said. "It is not a voluntary thing, led up to by pre-determination. There can be no question of making up. I never try to write nor to think. I do not invoke my own ideas. They spring into being of themselves, quite unsought. And, in a measure, they are uncontrollable."

My father was staring at me in silence.

"Eh?" he said merely as I paused.

I laughed.

"What I mean is, that a man, as a man, endowed with will, control, wishes, and so on, ceases to exist, you may say, while he is writing. He becomes then the tool of that peculiar, mysterious power that is moving in his brain. He writes as a clerk writes from dictation. He is the clerk pro tem of the impulse stirring his being, which dictates to him what it pleases. There is no consideration in his mind - 'I will write this or that' or 'I won't write the other.' He simply feels he must write a particular thing; it crowds off his pen before he can stop it. He does not know where, whence, how, or why the idea came to him. But it is there, clamouring to be written, and he writes it because he must. The expression, very often, of a thought is as uncontrollable as a physical spasm, and the man who writes it cannot always be held responsible for it."

"My dear Victor!"

"No, really," I said, laughing, "I am simply stating ordinary facts. I believe any writer, any acknowledged writer of talent, will bear me out, more or less. It is the old idea of inspiration - one cannot express it better - a breathing into. It is exactly that. The man of genius, in any form, feels at times-that is to say, when his fit is on, that there is a breathing into his brain. It becomes full of images he is unfamiliar with, crowded with thoughts that are quite foreign perhaps to the man himself, to his life, to his habits, and invested with a peculiar knowledge of things he has had no personal experience of. Then as suddenly as it came the fit goes; it is over, and he can write no more. Should he be so foolish as to try, his sentences become mere linked chains of nouns and verbs; his inspiration has gone. He cannot invoke it, cannot restrain it, cannot retain it, cannot recall it, and only very slightly control it."

"Ha!" said my father reflectively, going on with his soup, "deuced inconvenient."

"Inconvenient it may be," I said quietly. "All the same, that which is written under inspiration is the only stuff worth reading. The Greeks expressed the peculiar feeling that a man has when his inspiration comes upon him by the phrase, entheos eimi, and we can hardly find a better one, only unfortunately we don't believe in gods. Otherwise, entheos eimi contains everything, for the man who was only common clay before his inspiration, and will be common clay when it departs, feels, for the time, as if a god had descended, and was within him. And when, afterwards, he looks at what he has written he feels it is something not wholly his own, but that it is the work of some powerful influence he can hardly comprehend, and cannot certainly rule."

"But really I don't see that this has much relation to what I said about your writing something to please the British public!"

"It is the whole gist of the matter," I said. "I am proving to you that I am, to a certain extent, helpless in what I write; that it is impossible for me to think of publics, British or otherwise, of publishers or critics, when I am writing. I have no time to consider them, no space in my brain for them, no memory that such things, or anything outside of what I am describing, exists even. My only thought is to drive along my pen fast enough, in obedience to the strenuous impulse urging me. I do not 'make up,' as your phrase is, anything. I simply put down on paper, as fast as I can, the thoughts that are pouring into my brain, like the waves of a flood flowing over it. I am whirled away on the stream myself; my identity is lost, submerged. Now look here, I'll give you a cut and dried instance which will make clear how it is that I offend the prejudices, or the proprieties, or whatever you call it, in my books; at least I imagine it is in this way: Suppose I have a death scene to write. My MS. is waiting for that to complete it. I don't say to myself beforehand, Now there shall be a bed with Tomkins dying in it; there shall be Maria at the left-hand corner, and Jane at the right. The wife and doctor shall be grouped artistically at the foot. Tomkins shall make two speeches before he dies; no, three-three is more natural - uneven number. Now what shall Tomkins say? Yes. Ah - hum - what the deuce shall I make him say? It must not be too much like what a dying man would say, because the British public is dead against realism. It must not either show any strong contempt for religion; a little mild contempt, of course, goes down and is fashionable, but I must not express it forcibly. He must not either evince a disbelief in immortality - at least that's dangerous ground. Some publishers will accept it and some won't. - Better leave it out. Ah - hum - what shall Tomkins say? I have it! A retrospect of his past life! And yet - No, stay! that won't do. Something that sounds like something that might possibly be immoral might turn up in it, and that would be fatal - damn the MS. utterly. Well, look here, Tomkins has got to die, and I've got to finish the book, so I must get something down. 'Darling Mabel, this parting is terrible, but still I feel we shall meet in another world.' Now, is that safe? Has a similar phrase been put in heaps of novels before? Because the British public won't have anything too new. It likes to head over again what it has heard at least fifty thousand times before, and then it knows it won't be shocked. Yes, that sentence will do. Now I must put in a few more and then, thank goodness, the scene will be done! Now," I said, springing up from the table, "do you call that art? do you call it genius? Is a collection of bald phrases and second-hand sentiments, hooked together like that, worth anything when it's done?"

"My dear boy, don't excite yourself like that," my father answered deliberately. "Sit down and finish your soup."

"Oh, hang the soup!" I said, resuming my seat. "Shall I sound the gong? I have not told you my way yet, but I'm coming to it when the man's gone." I sounded the gong, and the butler came in with the next course.

There was no carving ever done at our table, so my father had only to tranquilly continue eating while I talked. He had forced me into the discussion, and now he should hear it to the end.

"Of course, if you do write the death of Tomkins like that you can keep your scenes orthodox, or whatever word you have in view. But, supposing my MS. is lying incomplete; - I have a conviction that I am going to write of death, but the method of the man's death is at present unknown to me, unthought of. - Then, some afternoon, I happen to be sitting smoking, and just perhaps wondering whether I shall go round to the club or not, when suddenly a scene, a death scene, the scene I have been waiting for, comes rushing through my head. It comes upon me with tremendous impetus; mechanically, almost unconsciously, I take up a pen and write. Space opens before me and I see a hospital ward. A blaze of light floods it. Rows of narrow beds are there, and on one I see Tomkins - dying. I make my way to him: now I am by his bed. I see him stretched beneath my eyes. I see the pillow dark with the sweat of his death agony - the night-shirt torn at his throat to get air. Have I time to consider then whether the British public like the word night-shirt, and whether it would not be safer to put

Tomkins into a dressing-gown? The man is there before me, dying, and he is in his night-shirt, and I must write it. Besides, my pen is tearing on. I cannot stop - he is dying. Will he speak before he dies? I do not know yet. His eyelids quiver, the black veins in his throat knot up, he gasps. I bend lower: 'his breath comes hurriedly: his eyes open and fix upon me: they are red, vitreous but conscious: then I know he will speak, he is going to - the next moment his half-strangled voice reaches my ear. He is speaking, and that which I hear him say, I write: no more, no less, no different. His voice dies away, inarticulate. I see his lips whiten and draw back upon his teeth. His hands clutch me as a convulsive spasm wrenches his muscles. There is a tense, rigid silence, and then one deep-drawn groan. Nerve, limb, muscle, and flesh collapse as the Life is set loose. The damp body sinks back, leaving its death sweat on my arms, its gasp in my ears. Tomkins is dead. But the impulse is not done with me yet. I cannot get out of that hospital ward till I have done everything, passed through all the circumstances that crop up naturally from the death of Tomkins. There is no ' making up.' The scene is being enacted before me. It is. It exists. It is the truth for the time being, and, as the truth, I write it. There is the miserable girl, sobbing convulsively, with her arms out-stretched in the bed-clothes. Can I leave her without some words of consolation? I must write down that she is there, because I see her there. There are some arrangements to be made with the nurse, and then, when I am leaving the ward, or at least intend to, my brain hurries the doctor up the ward to me. I don't ' make him up.' I had not the remotest idea of the head doctor appearing when I sat down to write. But now I see him approaching me between the beds, and before I can pass him, as I want to, he button-holes me and proceeds to explain that Tomkins never would have died if he had undergone an operation that the doctor had perceived from the very first moment was necessary. After a long talk with him, perhaps, my pen stops. I pause: and when I pause I know the inspiration has gone. As the ancients would say, the Muse or the God has departed and dictates no more. I fling aside the paper and look at my watch. Several hours passed in the hospital, but I'll go round to the club now. And I go. I know Tomkins is dead. It only occurs to me afterwards, as a secondary consideration, that in consequence the MS. is finished. Tomkins was not for the manuscript, but the manuscript for Tomkins. Now the point is - Can I be held responsible for that scene? It is not my fault that I have mentally seen a private soldier dying in hospital. The whole thing was involuntary."

"Very extraordinary views!" muttered my father.

I shrugged my shoulders in silence, and called up Nous to give him my untouched dinner.

"The best joke of it is, too," I said, suspending a strip of sirloin over the collie's nose, "the publishers admit if I had less talent they would print my things. I could not understand why my 'Laura Dean' was refused, so I went down to the publishers to try and find out. I saw the reader himself, and an awfully nice fellow he is, too. In reply to my question, he said the objection to the book was that it dealt with a wife leaving her husband. I stared at him in amazement. 'But, great Scott!' I said, 'that's a good old-fashioned theme enough. It's as old as the hills. It's the subject of - ' and I gave him a list of about a dozen eminent novels. 'Yes,' he admitted. 'But they are not written in the same way.' 'Is there anything coarse or low in the writing?' 'Oh, no! I should not say that!' 'Well, what is the matter with it, then?' 'The thing is too much brought before you. Of course, in these books you have mentioned the wife runs away, but it does not make much impression. You have put it all so forcibly, and given the characters and episode so much life, and driven the idea of her infidelity so far home to one, that, well, it becomes a different thing - one realises it.' 'Oh, then you admit the immoral theme and the language to be unobjectionable, and the book would have been accepted by the British public provided only it had been less well written?' 'Yes, I suppose it comes to that.' And then I caught his eye, and we both laughed. He is a clever fellow himself, I should think, and the ludicrousness of the idea tickled him as much as it did me. I came away. His admission was quite the truth. It is the British way to take the second-rate in every art and scout the best. Write a book poorly and feebly, and it passes. Write the same thing powerfully and well, and the cry is - It's improper! It's just the same thing in painting. Paint a nude woman snowy white, without a shade or a shadow, and looking altogether as no mortal woman ever did look, and the picture will be hung at the Academy, and people will say, 'How charming! So artistic!' But paint a woman with a glow on her neck and bosom, and the warm blood running in her arms, dare to make her a living, breathing thing on canvas, and your picture will be rejected. 'Excellent, unequalled, perfect, but - it cannot be seen!' And what is British art as a consequence? Justly is it looked down upon by the other nations. We simply set our heel upon the best men. And look at our productions! Look at the rot and the trash that floods the libraries every year! Look at the average novel! It's a disgrace to our intellect! Look at the woodeny dolls that are its men and women! And behold our Academy! See our pictures!"

"Don't rock your chair like that, Victor; it annoys me."

"Very good," I said, bringing my chair down on its fore legs again. "Are you ready for the cheese?"

"Yes; but won't you eat anything?"

"No, thanks. I am fed upon annoyance just now."

"You are getting thin on it, too," he answered, looking at me. "It's a pity you are so excitable!"

"It's a pity I was born in this confounded Britain! I should have got on all right with Parisian readers. But I don't despair even here. They can reject my MSS., but they can't take out my brains. I daresay I shall stumble across some man at last with courage enough to stand by me in the beginning and help me force open the British public's jaws and cram my ideas down its throat; and that once done, it will digest them perfectly, for it's a tough old beast, though very blind. Why on earth has that fellow carried off the champagne?"

"You finished the bottle yourself just this minute!" returned my father, in surprise.

"Did I? Oh, very likely! Absence of mind!"

"It seems to me if you had a little less of this talent you boast of you would be considerably the gainer."

"Possibly," I rejoined. "But a gift is a gift. You can't say to nature, take this back and let me have something more paying! Besides, I can't admit that for any earthly reason I would change. I have no desire to be a second-rate writer when I know I am a first!"

"By Jove! if conceit could carry the day!"

"No, there is no conceit," I persisted. "Is it conceit to say my hair is black? It is black, and everybody can see it is. I have nothing to do with it. Nature made it black, and black it is, and I know it. Should I gain anything by contending that it was red? I don't see that I should. However," I added, laughing, "The point is of no consequence. Put me down as a fifth-rate writer, if you like, until I become the fashion!"

"It does not seem you ever will, at this pace," he said quietly.

"Very good," I answered, equally quietly.

"Then you will not have the trouble of changing your opinion."

There was a long silence then. We each smoked without a word. At twenty minutes to ten my father got up. He always went to bed horribly early.

"What are you going to do, Victor?"

"I am going out," I answered, getting up and stretching myself.

"Will you be late?"

"Probably. I got no sleep last night, nor the night before. It's no earthly use my going to bed when I feel like this. I can't get to sleep by repeating hymns, as some fellow suggested the other day."

"Why don't you take morphia or something to help you?"

"I don't care to begin taking drugs," I said, "I would rather wear myself out, and induce sleep in that way. I shall take a three hours' walk or so."

"Well, good-night."

"Good-night."

When he was gone, I sat a few minutes in the easy chair, with my head in my hands thinking. I had meant to ask him a question at dinner, but that argument on talent had put it on one side. Well, it would do later.

"Coming out, Nous?" I said to the collie. The dog started and pricked his ears.

"Out?" I repeated, and he leapt to his feet and gave himself a joyful shake, and then stood on the hearth-rug in front of me, swaying slowly his great brush of a tail and poising his head at an intelligent angle. I got up, felt for my latch-key, and went into the hall. Nous waited impatiently while I put on my hat and overcoat, and then we went out together. The night was cold, wet, and foggy. It was late in November, and a light mist veiled the end of each black, deserted street.

I took no heed of anything, neither the atmosphere round me nor the direction in which my feet carried me. I was wrapped up in a maze of thoughts, and there was not a decently pleasant one in the whole lot.

They were warmed and brightened every now and then as a form that I loved glided amongst them, but even that form dragged after it a chain of painful, fettering considerations, and the gleams of light that it threw round it were only like those weak, pallid flashes of sun that flit through the clouds of thunder and storm in a hurricane.

CHAPTER II

The next morning when I came down to breakfast it was late, and my father had already withdrawn to his own library. I had missed again speaking to him, as I could not seek and disturb him there.

He also was a writer, though quite of a different school from myself. He wrote ardently upon politics, political economy, and statistics, things which I took no interest in.

The nation might arrange itself how it pleased for all I cared. What I wanted to arrange was my own life. I had no ambition to set my country's affairs straight, my own thoughts were too much engaged in tugging my own into some sort of order.

There were some letters for me, and I turned them over listlessly, balancing them tip in succession against the toast-rack in front of me, without opening any. The last I came to was quite different from any of the others, and being the last, it stood foremost before me, and I looked at it while I went on with my breakfast.

It is curious how representative a letter generally is of its writer. The mere outside is like a psychological photograph. Of course it does not give details, but it presents you with a wonderfully accurate outline of the cut of a person's identity. This envelope was square, and looked as hard, white and clean as if a stone-tablet had passed through the post. It bore a delicate, weak, feminine superscription, hurried and careless; the writing unformed, but graceful and distinguished; and on the other side of the letter, stamped in grey, stood a crest, and the motto subscrolled.

Yes, the woman who had written it was very like the letter. Immaculate and perhaps somewhat hard, delicate, and in will a little weak, impulsive and undecided, well-bred, and strikingly typical of the class to which she belonged.

I broke the letter open after a minute and read -

"DEAREST VICTOR, - Do come and see me as soon as you possibly can. A scheme for the next canvas occurred to me last night, but I want you to help me execute it. What about the manuscripts? If you can't come, tell me. Bring Nous. LUCIA."

I smiled as I replaced the letter. The composition was rather defective, and left the meaning decidedly indistinct. If I could not come I was to tell her. Tell her what? About the MS., or that I couldn't come?

And under what circumstances was I to take Nous? Apparently if I could not do so.

I was not sneering at the little note, and it went into my breast pocket, but it amused me.

"That is the way I ought to write for the British, I suppose?" I muttered, with a yawn. "Muddle all one's language up until nobody has the faintest idea of what the author's sentiments are, and then they don't know whether he means anything heterodox or not."

I got up. I might as well obey the orders I had just received.

There was a tired confusion of thought in my brain - a floating mass of half-formed embryonic ideas, wishes, plans and suggestions filled it that were quite useless for prompting or guiding any definite resolution as to what I should do in the immediate future.

Everything seemed to depend on something else, and it was impossible to find any positive basis upon which I could found a resolve.

If I could succeed as an author, my way was clear, but if I could not, and if . . . and if . . . And so on through a wearying, perplexing series of conditions.

Just then I felt unequal to regulating and giving order to this inward chaos, and I abandoned the attempt.

Meanwhile I would go over to the house in South Kensington, whence the letter had come.

It was about eleven when I arrived there, and I was told Miss Grant was "upstairs, as usual."

I nodded, and went up the necessary six flights of stairs to a familiar landing on the third floor.

A door in front of me stood ajar, and with a sign to Nous to remain on the stairs, I knocked at it.

There was no answer and no sound from within, and thinking the room was empty after all, I pushed the door wide and went in.

It was a huge room, used as a studio, facing the north light, and with three large windows.

Before the middle one there was an easel, and the girl was in the room, standing there in front of the canvas between me and the light. She was seemingly entirely abstracted and absorbed. She was completely motionless, and for the moment she communicated her stillness to me.

I paused, silent, looking at her.

She was standing directly in front of me, facing the canvas, that was perfectly blank at present.

One hand rested on her hip, the other was raised and pressed to her head, as when a person looks into distance, and the arm and elbow and wrist traced a delicate curve against the dull grey square of London window pane.

A twist of hair about as thick as my arm fell nearly to her waist. It was decidedly not gold; that is, it did not suggest dye and the Haymarket; but it was fair and curly, and seemed to hold light imprisoned amongst it.

The figure was tall, and erred, perhaps, on the side of slightness.

Certainly it would have been too slight for those men whose scale of admiration runs - so much in the pound. But the architecture of the form was perfect. Each line was worthy of study in itself as a thing of beauty, and the harmony of them all in the whole figure, whether it moved or was at rest, gave an indefinable pleasure to the eye.

What a lovely thing it was this form, seeming to hold in itself the light and pleasure and glow of life, as it stood, the only brilliant thing in that cold north room.

And it might be mine, might have belonged to me long since if . . . well if . . . that was just it.

I made a step forward and she turned.

"Oh, I'm so glad you've come," she said, laying her hand in mine. "I want you so much."

We shook hands.

Although we were cousins, and had been engaged for the last two years, this was our invariable method of greeting and leave-taking.

I had never kissed her, nor was I sure whether I ever really desired to.

There were times when the thought that precedes the impulse or the impulse that gives birth to the thought came to me, but always when I was away from her and not with her, and consequently the desire culminated in nothing.

When I was actually beside her all my own feelings seemed suddenly held in suspension, just as one stops with feet chained when one discovers one has come abruptly upon sacred ground.

There had been times when I had hurried to this girl with words eager to be spoken on my lips, and at the first sight of her they had died unuttered on my tongue, just as words die into silence in the presence of a somnambulist.

"Why am I specially necessary?" I said, smiling, as we stood in front of the easel. "Will you let me paint you as Hyacinthus?" I went into a fit of laughter. "My dear girl! anything to oblige you, but consider," I said, looking down into her eager eyes; "you ought not to have a model of six-and-twenty. Hyacinthus was probably sixteen."

"You don't know how old he was!" she said, mockingly, her azure, sunny eyes lighting up with laughter, too, as she leant on the bending maul-stick and looked up at me.

"No, I don't know," I answered; "but I can infer it. If we only went upon what we actually know we should not go very far."

"Well, he might have been as much as nineteen, and you don't look quite six-and-twenty; and the remaining difference I can soften down. Have you any other excuse to make to get out of the bother of sitting?"

"You are a horrid little wretch to put it like that," I answered, "and I won't say another word of advice. Paint your Greek youth as you please. Of course, you'll give him this mustache with waxed ends? It's very appropriate!"

"No; of course I shan't. Now, Victor, do be sensible. You can be so nice at times!"

"Can I really? You are kind!"

"I want to hear about the manuscript. Was it accepted?" she said very gently, with her hand on mine.

"Well, that's soon told," I answered. "It wasn't."

She said nothing. Probably she knew that the mere expression "I am sorry" would be inadequate to say to a man who felt every failure as keenly as I did, and I hastened to remove her difficulty.

"Don't let us talk of it," I said. "Tell me of the new conception."

"It is to be called 'The Death of Hyacinthus,'" she said, glancing at the vast, vacant canvas, on which, doubtless, her eye saw the whole vision already. "The scene is to be flooded with sunlight, that pours in upon a green, open glade. The life-sized figure of Hyacinthus will be standing three-quarters towards the spectator, and a little towards the rush of light from the setting sun. His eyes are to be fixed upon the quoit which will be here, at this end of the canvas, opposite him. It will be tinged blood-red in the sun's rays, and seem a little above him."

She paused, with her eyes on the canvas. She had drifted away on the stream of her idea. "And what about the two gods?" I asked.

She started.

"Oh yes, I was going to tell you. Zephyrus will only be represented by the effect of the wind seen on the bushes, on the trees, and every blade of grass or fern in the picture. These small tamarisk trees that fringe the glade will be bent nearly double. The spirit of the wind must be in the whole painting. That will be the great effect, of course."

"And Apollo?"

"I cannot put him in. You see, I do want this to be taken at the Academy next year, and though they have scores of nude women, they would not have a nude god at any price: and it would be too inartistic to clothe Apollo. So I have supposed him invisible; being a god, he would be so to all except Hyacinthus. Simply his hand, holding the quoit, will be faintly suggested, and the light allowed to fall through it."

There was silence. "Do you like it?" she said suddenly to me.

"Yes. I think the idea is unconventional: but on that account you will probably be rejected."

"I must risk it. Hyacinthus is to be in white, and must look radiantly, gloriously happy."

"I say, do you want me to look radiantly, gloriously happy- because that will be rather difficult just now."

"As far as you can. You see, the point is that he was struck and killed in the moment of supreme confidence and light-hearted joy."

"How very uncomfortable! Is that to be my fate?" I said laughing.

"Well, will you, Victor?"

"Will I what?"

"Take your seat here, now, and let me sketch you?"

"Certainly; but I thought you said he was to be standing?"

"I don't think I can take you for the whole figure. You are too much occupied to be able to spare the time. And I can find another model for the figure. I should like to take you for the whole, but you may be going away or something before the painting is finished. But in any case I have set my heart on giving him your head and neck."

"You flatter me awfully," I returned. "You shall have them - but that wretched Nous is outside all this time. May I let him in?"

"Oh yes! I did not know you had brought him!" she exclaimed, and ran herself to the door and called him in.

He came in meekly. And I stood where she had left me by the easel, and watched her bend over him and caress him, and I thought I was badly used.

"Now, will you sit there?" she said, coming back and indicating a chair.

I took it in silence. Then she paused, looking at me.

"What is it?" I said, enquiringly.

"Would you - " and she hesitated.

"Continue: command me."

"Could you take off your collar?"

"I think, perhaps, I could," I said, looking up into her serious face. "I am not aware that it is an absolute fixture!"

She laughed, but she was seldom chaffed out of a reply.

"It might have been in one with the shirt!" she said.

"Far-seeing intuitiveness! I admit it might; but fortunately in this case it's not. Then you'll excuse me if I take off my coat?"

"Yes, I want you to - coat, collar, and tie; so that I can sketch your neck down to the base of the throat."

"Ah!" I said, drawing off my coat, "I was wondering how you were going to fix up Hyacinthus with a lavender tie!"

She deigned no answer to that, and sat down just in front of me. A piece of plain drawing paper was put upon the easel before the canvas.

"Will you raise your head more? and throw your eyes up? higher, above my head!"

"May I not look straight at you?"

"No: up! up! to the window above me!"

"Won't you come and put me in the right position?"

"No. I am sure you have intellect enough to understand verbal directions."

"Well there," I said, throwing myself into the position she wanted; "that is easy: but how about that jolly expression? where's that to come from?"

"Can't you imagine for a moment that you are successful, and we are married?"

"A pretty good stretch of the imagination that!" I muttered, "as things are at present!"

And involuntarily I brought my eyes down from the window to the pale, delicate, abstracted face opposite me. I did not intend to convey any reproach to her, but perhaps she thought so, for she seemed to answer that which she took to be in my mind.

"But, Victor, you know," she said, laying down the pencil she had just taken up, "it is in your own hands. I am willing to marry you when you like!"

She said it very gently, but with just a touch of cold restraint that irritated me excessively.

"Oh yes, I know it's all my own confounded fault, but that does not make it any pleasanter. However, let all that pass. I'll look as cheerful as I can."

There was a long silence. She was absorbed in the drawing, and I in my own thoughts, as I stared through the upper pane, as directed, at the grey, drifting, hurrying November clouds. Had I descried a quoit there about to descend upon me I should have been rather pleased than not. At last I became conscious of an intolerable crick in my neck.

"May I move?"

"Oh, one minute! one minute!" she answered, and her voice struck me. It was faint, breathless, mechanical: the voice of a person whose whole being is tense with some straining effort. At least fifteen more minutes of silence passed.

"I say! I really must turn my head now!"

"No, no! not for worlds! Keep still!"

I kept still, but I felt sick with the peculiar cramp in my neck. Suddenly she dropped the crayon and started up.

"Now you may move, Victor! I've finished!"

I brought my head down to its ordinary level with considerable thankfulness, and as my eyes fell upon her I was rather startled. Her figure seemed expanded as she stood, and the white serge of her bodice rose and fell heavily. All the blood had flowed from her face, leaving it blanched, colourless. In her eyes the azure iris had disappeared, the dilated pupils had brimmed over it, and left nothing behind the lashes but shining, liquid blackness. Unconsciously, seemingly, her left hand was pressed to her left side, beneath the heart, and I saw it tremble; and the whole form quivered as she leaned slightly forward with her gaze bent upon the canvas. There was for the time being some great force lent her. Some power had stirred in the brain, and now seemed overflowing through the physical system - doubtless at its expense. This was inspiration, certainly, and valuable for its creative power, but the merely physical life and physical frame panted and fainted after its painful throes to produce that which the brain commanded. I looked at the girl, oblivious of me, oblivious of herself and of the pain that forced her hand mechanically to her side - looked half with pleasure, half with alarm. It must always bring a delight to the human being to watch the triumph of intellect over matter, of the mental over the physical system, of the mind over the body. The sympathy of our own mind must go with the fellow-mind in its struggles for freedom. It is like one captive calling to another from behind his prison bars. But when we love the body too, and when our reason tells us that the striving captive, if set free, must die; when we remember that by some horrible, unnatural anomaly this spirit, that at times seems divinity itself, is condemned to live in this abominable prison and to perish there, with and in its fetters, then the wave of exultant pleasure, of exuberant, arrogant triumph, that swept over us, poor fellow-prisoners, watching those fetters shaken and almost cast off, thunders back upon us, turned into the bitterest humiliation. I felt it all - the pitiable mockery of man's nature, the inexplicable, terrible union of a god and a brute in one frame, and the god dependent on the brute, and both mortal - as I looked at the slight, lovely form of the woman I loved, and saw it rocked and swayed, and left pained and breathless with the struggles of the powers within to assert and express themselves. It had so happened that I had never seen her at work before. It was only recently that she had been allowed to give up set studies for her own creative fancy. For years she had been employed in acquiring the technique of her art; and even beside these considerations, I had not been with her in her moments of most tense application, and I should not have been with her now but that I was needed as a tool in the work. And as I saw her at this moment, filled with mental energy and dominated by the pleasure of mental labour, a quick sympathetic elation came over me, almost immediately after to be replaced by simple fear.

"I am afraid you have overtaxed yourself rather," I said, in conventional phrase; "I'm afraid you're in pain."

"Oh, that's nothing! Come and tell me what you think!" she said, extending her hand, but not taking her eyes from the drawing. "This is only the first study, of course. But tell me, have I got a sufficiently - well - expectant - rapt expression? I am not quite sure."

I saw she was too utterly preoccupied to attend to anything I said of herself then, so I did not insist farther, and went up to the easel. I was not an artist nor a critic, nor in any way qualified to be a judge of painting as painting; but of genius, who is not a judge? In any art it is recognisable, patent, obvious to all. There is no human clod, no boor who is utterly insensible to its influence. It needs no education to perceive its presence, though the ignorant could not tell you what that presence was. Genius is as the sun itself: as universally perceptible. Even the rustic clown feels the sun hot upon his face. Ask him what sun is, and he cannot say, but he feels the difference between sun and no sun. And the power in this rough drawing beat in upon my perceptions as the sun beats on the labourer's face.

"I think it's a triumph," I answered. "You have caught a most startling look of concentration."

"I am so glad!" she said, lightly.

The strain was over, and she was descending into ordinary mundane life again, but the hand she had put on my arm chilled through the shirt sleeve like ice.

"Do you recognise yourself?"

"Ye - es," I said, slowly; "except for that very glorified nose you've given me!"

She laughed, and moved the paper off the easel.

"Now I just want to give you an idea of how the tamarisk will be swayed," she said, holding a crayon between her tiny white teeth, and motioning me to a couch under the window. "Sit down there and wait a minute. I'll just sketch them roughly for you to get an approximation."

I sat down on the couch facing her, and occupied myself by replacing my collar, etc. The studio was fireless and uncommonly chilly. Then I leaned back and studied the girl as she sat there, one little foot crossed over the other, and a piece of millboard supported on her raised knee. The tamarisk seemed to call for little expense of the divine energy, for she was as tranquil, smiling, and human as usual, now, as she sketched the bushes. They were far more mechanical work, naturally, than creating an expression and throwing it on a human face. The light from the window behind me fell full upon her, and seemed positively to brighten in her proximity. I wonder how, in their canons of beauty, the Latins could possibly have inscribed Frons minima, underrating the forehead, the sublimest feature in the human face, the great distinction between our countenance and that of our Simian prototypes. In this woman I thought it was, perhaps, her chief attraction. Round the temples and summit her light hair lay in thick loose curls. It did not "stray" anywhere. On the contrary, it was very intelligent hair, and knew exactly what to do with itself, how to curl upwards here and catch the light, how to cluster together there in adorable circles and half-circles in the shadow. And then came her forehead, a smooth band of white velvet, upon which two bow-like eyebrows were delicately traced. Excepting these and the vivid blue colouring in the eyes, and the rose and white tinting of the flesh, she had no positive beauties. The nose was a straight little nose, but very English, not the least sculptural, and the lips were rather too thick. They looked best when she was speaking, and their crimson was divided, and showed the small, even teeth behind them. Sitting watching her, now that her face was no longer flushed and animated in conversation, I noticed it looked white and tired, and all round the eyes were faint, discoloured shades. She looked overworked: looked as I myself looked in the early morning when I went upstairs from a night's work in my study to dress for breakfast.

"What were you doing last night?" I asked, abruptly. If I interrupted the work on the bushes, no matter; she must work less.

She looked up with a sudden flush.

"How did you know?" she answered, looking at me with confusion and perplexity in her eyes.

"I know nothing. I merely ask you. You were up all night?"

Her face became quite pale again, and she raised her eyebrows with a slight smile of indifference.

"Yes, I was."

I paled too, with annoyance.

"Lucia! this is the one thing I asked you to do for me; to give your nights, at least, to rest!"

"I know you did," she said, passionately, looking at me, her lips quivering and her face growing paler and paler. "But it is impossible sometimes! What gain is there in discussing these things? A perfect scheme came to me last night, and I sat here thinking of it - planning it upon this canvas. I could not have slept had I left this room. Besides, to close your brain to your ideas when they do come! - it is madness! I might never have seen the picture so vividly before me again if I had not stayed to think it out, to realise it, to impress it, as it were, clearly on myself. I cannot promise you, Victor - I never have, I would not before - to go to bed and try to sleep when a plan occurs to me suddenly for a canvas, as it did last night!"

"But think of sitting in a room like this all night with no fire! This studio is positively freezing!"

"Is it? I don't feel it."

"No. That is what I complain of. You feel nothing and think of nothing while you are at work, and you will injure yourself unconsciously. If you do these things you will certainly break down."

She merely shrugged her shoulders and looked past me through the window, an arrogant determination filling her blue eyes. The next minute she was speaking rapidly, and with an intonation of impatience in her voice.

"You know I am given over to the work - entirely, utterly. It is useless to expect me to sacrifice it to anything. On the contrary, everything must be sacrificed to it. Health, life itself, must be in the second place. I only value my life for the sake of this talent. Of course, I know if I lose my life I lose it too; but, equally, I can produce nothing without work. If I am to succeed I must work simply - it is necessity."

Each word was incisive, and seemed to cut slightly like falling steel from those soft, warm lips. A sudden desire rushed through me to teach her - at any rate, to exert myself to the utmost to teach her - that her life was valuable to her for other things than the capacity it gave to work. But I checked the words and the thoughts that rose, acting on the same principle as had guided me hitherto. To wake her to a sense of the pleasure and the gifts life holds, without being able to confer either - that could not be any gain. I merely said:

"And if you give up your life for the sake of this painting, Lucia, is that fair to me?"

"You would have your work," she answered.

The tone was cold and calm, and she went on sketching.

"Do you think that would console me?"

"I do not think: I am convinced of it. You are a man to whom your work, your genius, is everything. This holds the first, the ruling place in your life, and will always do so. I am in the second, I believe; but it is the second, and the step between is wide. It is quite right it should be so. I am not complaining, but it is useless to deny that it is so. Well, when one loses but the second object in one's life -"

A soft smile swept over her face, and she lifted the white lids and dark lashes - that had been drooped as she looked down at the drawing paper - with a brilliant, mocking flash in her eyes. I met them, and though I was not looking at it, but directly back into her eyes, the whole charming figure forced itself upon my vision. The round throat and the fine shoulders and the delicate curves of the long figure, sloping to the waist beneath the white serge bodice. Had she really but a second place? If I realised at any time I was not to possess her after all, what then? Should I be consolable? An angry denial leapt to my lips. There was no question of first or second. These two passions for this woman and for my own success were coordinate forces, and their very equality it was that kept me passive, without decisive action between them.

There was a sort of confusion in my brain - a longing to make some protestations. The words crowded excitedly to my lips, but I kept them closed. The conversation was on dangerous, critical ground. If I began to speak now, in this frame of mind,

I did not know what I might say. My own brain was not sufficiently clear and collected. I did not know myself quite how far that which she had said was the truth. It is useless to talk vaguely and at random, or on mere passing sensations of the moment. Before speaking to another, before entering on a discussion, one must know exactly what one is saying - be prepared to act in accordance with every statement, and accept and realise the responsibility of each word, and all this at that moment I was not, - far from it. I felt my thoughts disordered and confused. Before my mental eye swam a mist of manuscript; before my physical eye rose and fell that gently beating breast. I took out my watch.

"It's a quarter past twelve, Lucia," I said, rising; "I must go."

The girl started to her feet and came in front of me.

"Victor, are you offended at what I said?"

I looked down at her with a slight smile.

"I am not so easily offended," I said, quietly.

"I will talk about all these things with you another day - not now."

"And do forgive me for siting up at nights. I know you do not like it. I know it ruins my looks, but I must work. Besides, all my excitement, all my amusement, is in it too. When I am not with you it is all I have. It is different for you, as a man, besides your work and besides myself, you have all sorts of distractions and -"

"What sort of distractions do you think I have?" I asked, quietly, and looking straight into her eyes.

Her words might mean and include a very great deal.

"Oh, how can I say! When you feel restless and unable to work at seven in the evening, say from then till seven the next morning your time is your own - balls, the Empire; there are a thousand things - all the pleasure, or at any rate the passing excitement that you can take in these ways, I crush into the excitement that there is in work - in overwork."

There was nothing in the actual words, but I felt the thoughts that underlay them, unexpressed. I resented the opinion she held of me. It was untrue, and I meant to remove it. I was silent an instant, thinking how to find words passably comprehensible and yet conventionally circumlocutory and euphemistic. After a moment I said simply -

"If you think I am leading a fast life, it is a mistake. I am not. What makes you think I have distractions, as you put it?"

"Oh, nothing, except that I know you are constantly not at home at - in the evenings. But really, Victor - " she added, a scarlet flush leaping across her face, and then leaving it pale and cold, with a shade of reserve and pride upon it. "I have no wish to approach this subject at all. I should never think of enquiring into or interfering with a man's life. These are things that must rest in his own hands."

I looked at her, as the graceful figure seemed to expand with pride, at the dignity of each line of her form and the pose of the distinguished head, and an irritated flush crept into my own face.

"I am out constantly, as you say," I answered, "because I cannot sleep, but I walk then simply in search of fatigue. Pleasure, Lucia! there can be none for me now until you belong to me. As for my life, it is a hard-working and as absolutely without relief as your own - absolutely."

She was silent.

"You don't believe me?"

"Of course I believe you," she answered, impulsively, putting her white hand suddenly into mine. "If you say so, but -"

"But what?"

She hesitated and coloured. I had not the least idea of what she was really going to say. I thought the "but" led to some condition more or less contradictory to her expression of belief in me, or, perhaps, to some statement she had heard, or something that she had thought. And I pressed her.

"But what?" I repeated.

"I was going to say, I have no wish to make your life harder than it is. I do not want our engagement to impose impossible laws upon you, nor do I set up an imaginary standard for you. You have your honour and your own self-respect, and I know I shall always be satisfied with the standard you raise for yourself."

The voice was very soft, and her touch and eyes caressing. She had not said in the least what I had expected, and she had touched, as she always did in me, the best springs in my thoughts. Her own pride, and her unquestioning assumption of mine, stung all that I had.

"Even you, Lucia, could not have a higher!" I answered on the impulse.

She smiled.

"That is exactly what I say," she said, and the smile went on into a slight laugh. "When will you come again to sit for Hyacinthus?"

"To-morrow, at the same time! Will that do?"

"Yes. It's immensely good of you. How can I thank you?"

I looked down at the red lips, at the delightful neck and shoulders, for a second in silence, then I pressed her hand, whistled to Nous, and went out. As soon as I had passed down the stairs and reached the street the bitter rush of feelings that the sight of this girl roused in me, and that her actual presence held in check, swept over me unrestrained. Why had I left her like that? I asked myself savagely. Why had I not drawn her into my arms and kissed her till all that soft delicate face was one flame of scarlet? Then a contemptuous smile came with the answering thought. What use were mere empty kisses if she gave me a thousand! This state of things could not go on. The life that I led seemed growing more and more unendurable week by week. It was a life of perpetual restraint, of refusal to every wish, of denial to every desire that rose in me, in which there was a bar laid upon every impulse, and an immovable chain upon every tendency. I was ambitious, and I could get no recognition. I was gifted, at least in my own estimation, and I could force open no field for my gifts. I was in love, and there was no means of attaining its object. Patience! patience! This was what I had been saying to myself hour by hour for two years, but there were times when it seemed that my brain, my whole system, was collapsing in the nervous irritation, in the chafing and the straining of this existence, which was filled with nothing but successless work, continuous disappointment, and unsatisfied desires.

Night succeeded night in which sleep was an impossibility, when my head seemed light and turning as in delirium with the violence and intensity of longing to shape my life differently. Could I have obtained the fulfilment of one desire or of the other, the strength of my nature would have flowed naturally into the channel opened before it. Could I have seen my work succeeding I would have foregone everything else willingly and worked with satisfied ardour, closing my eyes to the pleasure of life. Could I have obtained Lucia I would have been content to work and wait patiently till success chose to come to me. But the latter desire depended on the former, and when I thought of Lucia, her image only brought back upon me the stunning, deadening sense of the necessity of success, and so my thoughts were dragged round in a perpetual, wearying, dizzying circle, like a fixed wheel revolving without motion forward.

I had grown to hate my present daily existence. It was a state of enforced passive inaction that seemed corroding my nerves as the long worn fetter eats into the flesh. The current of life was running at its swiftest and fiercest in my veins. Vitality was ardent in the brain and blood, but there was no worthy expense of my energies, and they simply fell back upon themselves again and again, thwarted, baffled, unused, until existence seemed an intolerable curse. I saw daily other men's works accepted and received, and their talent and genius praised that could produce such a work, which, when it drifted into my hands, I recognised was no better than the MSS. lying in my study, unused, wasted. Sometimes the morning of a day would pass in looking through the reviews and criticisms of the favourite novel of the hour, the afternoon in reading the book itself and forming a judgment of it, and then an evening of sickly irritation would follow, in which, pacing backwards and forwards, in the empty study, I had to admit that the author, no more gifted, no more favoured with talent than myself, had been successful and I had not. The very praise I received for my powers from men who would not help me to employ them was a maddening stimulus.

"Talent? Yes, decidedly, but too heterodox for us."

This was the general resume of the opinion of the publishing world that had determined to eject me and shut its door in my face. Had it been hinted that the rejection was on the ground of incapacity it would have been easier to bear, but, without exception, every declined manuscript had been accompanied with a warm commendation of the art that the critic chose to think was so misapplied. Often, walking up and down the length of that study with these letters of empty compliment crowding the mantelpiece, I felt like a captured tiger in a cage, being goaded and thrust at through the bars. And, together with this excessive longing of the brain to employ its power raged the useless, vehement desire for the woman, until in those moments of silent solitude, it seemed as if two living vultures were upon me, slowly tearing me asunder. As I walked away from Lucia this morning, and when I reached my own steps, I was conscious of a sense of physical illness; my head seemed light and dizzy, as when one gets up after long fever. I was so long opening the door that Nous, who had pushed his whole body close up against it, looked at me with surprise. As we went in I had one clear determination, and that was to apply once more to my father for help. He could, if he would, enable me to marry Lucia. Success must come with time. It was this time that would be transformed. This time, this daily life of waiting work, that hung upon me now like a wolf, with its fangs, gnawing my brain, would then, if I possessed her, pass by like a dove upon wings. After luncheon, when he was standing by the hearth, I thought, was a good time to approach the subject, and I came up to the other end of the mantelpiece.

"Don't you think you could," I said, striking a lucifer and lighting up a cigar, without the least wish to smoke at that moment, "manage to let Lucia and myself arrange something?"

He looked at me a little ironically.

"Have you heard that the firm have rescinded their decision, and are going to bring out the book after all?" he asked quietly.

I coloured with anger and annoyance at the sneer. "No," I answered, simply, "I have not."

"Then, my dear Victor, you know it is quite useless to re-open this old question. I have told you before, and I can only repeat it now, I am not going to make you an independent allowance, that you may marry your cousin and comfortably settle down into a do-nothing existence."

"I never propose such an existence," I answered calmly. "Have I ever led it? am I leading it now?"

"No, because just now you have every incentive to work, and you have all your energies turned in that one direction, but with a secured income, independence, and married to this girl, I know exactly what you would become, and if I can prevent it, I am not going to have my son a confirmed idler about town."

"I can't think how you can so misjudge me," I said. "If you would make me an allowance - say 300 Pounds Sterling a year - half the rent of this house we live in!" I added bitterly. "I should marry Lucia, but on that account I should not neglect the work. Incentive! I should have every inducement to work then as now! - if inducement were necessary - Which it is not. I work now, not because I am driven by motives and wishes, but because to write is as natural to me as to sleep or breathe!"

"Please remember you are talking to a sane Englishman," he answered coldly; "and if you want me to listen to you, you must talk sense."

"Very good," I said, bringing my teeth down nervously on the cigar. "Put it entirely on the ground of motive if you like; I should want to succeed then doubly, and success is only a thing of time. It will come one day to me, as it has come to others who have had the same difficulties at first."

My father smiled sceptically.

"We shall see. In any case, if you are so certain of success, you can't object to the fulfilment of your wishes resting on so sure a contingency!"

"That has nothing to do with it. I did not say how long success might not be deferred, and I am unwilling to wait in these circumstances."

"Ah! - delightful frankness!" he returned derisively, and I looked away from him into the fire.

It shot across me then, amongst my own worrying thoughts, how strange it is that one human being should have so little sympathy with another, that where one can, without the least annoyance to himself, confer all that another desires, there seems always some inexplicable impulse to withhold it. And I - if I had power to give, if I ever possessed money, it should be to give, give freely and without conditions to those who needed it.

Perhaps my father guessed what I was thinking of. At any rate, he recommenced the conversation by saying -

"You have had a great deal done for you, Victor, though you may consider yourself very ill-used. You had a most expensive education. Then you passed into the army - brilliantly, I admit, but you were aided in every possible way. Then you had a fancy to go to India. Well, I got your regiment changed, and you went. Six months after you write that you have determined to become an author. I assent to that, much against my judgment, and you send in your papers. Good. What have you done since then? Nothing but write things no one will print, and hang about your cousin!"

A dull anger lit up in all my veins, and sent the blood to my head at his words. Still, they were practically the truth, and I knew I had no right to resent them.

"Now," he continued, "I make you a reasonable and just proposal, and you know that it is so. I give you every opportunity to display your talent, if you have any, which I very seriously doubt. You have leisure and unlimited means at your disposal. I only stipulate that before I make you independent, and before you marry, you shall give some proof of your powers in literature. I don't say you must wait till you have acquired a fortune. Your first production that is accepted and acknowledged sets you free. When I see you are really on the way to a profession, I will take care your finances don't trouble you, and as to marriage, you can then, of course, do what you please. But as to assisting you now to hurry into an affair that I don't under any circumstances particularly approve of - No."

"Why don't you approve of it?" I said, with a faint smile; "if I were in love with a housemaid or a ballet dancer I could understand your objection, but a girl in our own rank, educated, pretty, clever - what more would you have?"

My father shrugged his shoulders and elevated his eyebrows, and finally answered - "I should have liked a little more sanity between you. Remember there is insanity on her side and insanity on yours, and you both of you seem half-cracky already, to my mind. Then you are cousins. The relationship is near, unpleasantly near. You are both very much alike, extremely excitable, and with both your heads stuffed full of nonsense. She is exceedingly delicate, and no wonder, sitting up all night sketching and sitting in all day painting! I wish you could have chosen some strong, sensible, matter-of-fact young woman!"

I smiled as I listened. The combination of those three adjectives fairly set my teeth on edge, and suddenly I seemed to see Lucia's pale brilliant face, with its dilated eyes and genius-lit pupils, swimming in the shaft of sunlight that fell between us on the rug.

"What the children of two such maniacs will be, I tremble to think of!" he said after a minute.

I laughed outright, flung my cigar end into the fire, and stretched myself.

"I don't think you need trouble about the children!" I said significantly.

His remark sounded so ludicrous to me that my answer came spontaneously, but it was the worst thing I could have said. My father's old-fashioned ideas were the rock upon which we invariably split. Otherwise we should have got on very well.

But he was entirely of the school of yesterday, and I was entirely of the school of to-morrow. His forehead contracted violently, and he said curtly -

"Now, don't let me hear any of that ridiculous nonsense you were talking the other day! I won't have these sentiments expressed in my hearing!"

I laughed, and said nothing. I never wish to express sentiments in anybody's hearing that they don't want.

"Of course," he said, finally, after a long pause, "you can please yourself. If you like to try and find a situation as clerk or secretary or shoe-black, and marry this girl on the proceeds, do so. But if you do, you will get no help from me in future. Don't come to me then for funds to bring out your MSS. If you choose to disgrace your family and disappoint my expectations, consider yourself entirely cut off from me, that's all."

There was another stretch of silence, and then -

"Well, which is it to be, Victor? Lucia or Genius?"

"I really hardly know," I answered, lightly. "I want them both. I'll think it over."

And with Nous, who had sprung to his feet as I moved, closely following me, I crossed the dining-room and went out, upstairs to my own writing and sitting-room. Here I flung myself into an arm-chair and let my hand hang over the side and rest on the collie's neck. And as I curled absently the locks of fur round my fingers, the thought came - When would my hand play as familiarly with those short, glistening curls on Lucia's forehead? Of course, as far as that went, we were engaged, and I might have put our relations on a far more intimate and familiar footing than they were now. I might have kissed her, twisted and untwisted that great cable of hair, put my arm round her waist, and so on and so on. No one would have objected since we were fiances and, in addition, cousins. And it is difficult to define exactly the impulse that had prompted me to abstain from all of these things. Partly it was an impulse in her defence, and partly in my own. I felt that it was difficult enough, hard enough, to keep in perfect control my own passionate impulses when I was with her, even now, while there was the screen and shield between us of her abstracted calm; when there was a certain coldness and reserve around her; when there was no beginning, no opening, no invitation of demonstration; when her complete unconsciousness of herself helped me to restrain and conceal all my own feelings; but if this were dispelled; if she came to greet me with the bright conscious flush of passion; if I saw reflected in her eyes the fire that burnt in me; if I were permitted to take her into my arms and cheat myself for a single illusive instant with the thought that she was mine - what would it all mean? Only giving a sharper, more cutting edge to the bit in my mouth and rousing in her a hunger I could not satisfy. She was at present devoted to her art with a devotion that left her practically indifferent to everything else, and there was a thin frame of ice round her, which her abstraction and her ceaseless work built up; but I was convinced that the smouldering fire of a woman's nature lay underneath - that it was concealed never cheated me for an instant into the belief it was not existent. She was pure - perfectly, absolutely immaculate; but there was another power within and transfused throughout her innocence that swayed and subdued my will as innocence alone could never do. She reminded me of some exquisite, delicate porcelain flagon filled with sparkling wine, that sends its hot crimson glow through the snowy transparent tints of its circling walls. The wine within lies, at present, in glowing tranquillity, unshaken and unstirred, and the beauty and the purity of the flagon grows upon one as one looks. One would hesitate certainly to stretch an unclean hand to lift it, hesitate to touch it with lips that were not pure - but as certainly one sees that, if hand and lip are clean, and one may raise it to oneself, there is intoxication within that cup. Though its brilliant walls are white, they are not so because they hold thin water or turgid milk or yet vacancy. Of the nature of porcelain, they are clear and brilliant, for as such they left the potter's hands; but that faint flush stealing through them tells us that that within is wine. And as the purity of a cup like this is different from that of a clean, thick, common china cup standing empty on the board, so was Lucia different from the ordinary virtuous English girl. And for her I would do and suffer much, and feel glad in it. I looked upon her as this vase, and since I had known her I had kept my hand clean, that one day I might take it without remorse. And in my treatment of herself I acted as I did because I saw that, as yet, her passions and her nature slumbered, just as the wine, unshaken, is steady within the cup.

Now, in my present helpless condition, to merely wake and rouse them, to distract and disturb her, and lift her out of her art, to draw her half from her own life, before I could take her wholly into my own, seemed a sacrilegious cruelty. And this was why, from the commencement of our engagement, I had said to myself - On this one condition only.

This was why, on the evening when I put the circlet of the engagement ring over the delicate finger, I had not touched the lips thanking me. I knew I could not kiss her coldly. These things depend upon one's nature. Some men shake hands listlessly. I cannot. If I take a friend's hand I grasp it warmly. How then, here, with those passive lips under mine, could I prevent them from drawing in the enthusiasm from my own? And this once done, I did not know how it might stir in her, and break up her life and turn her aside from the tranquil path of abstraction and occupation she was following now. I am not saying that, as a rule, a woman waits for her lover's kiss to arouse her. On the contrary, I am well aware that most women are uncommonly wide-awake from their thirteenth year, and it is a very old-fashioned and quite exploded idea to suppose that the springs of their nature lie dormant until one particular individual unlocks them. I am only saying that this girl was as yet entirely given over to her genius, and happy in it; and I loved her too well to weaken an impulse towards art which she could gratify, and create an impulse towards love which I could not for so long satisfy. So with all this in my brain, and with a guard upon myself that had never been relaxed since, I released her hand, with my ring upon it, as gently as I had taken it, and the quiver of nervous, painful excitement, that had shot through me as she laid it on my knee confirmed my resolution. Why teach her also, one moment before she need know it, the pain of self-repression?

"Is it not pretty," she had said.

"Which, the hand or the ring?"

"Why, the ring, of course," she had said, laughing. "You are too bad, Victor!"

"I don't know. I think the hand is decidedly the lovelier. But the ring is useful as a sign that now there is but one man in the world for you, as, Lucia, there is for me henceforth but one woman."

She had looked up suddenly, and her eyes had met mine with the passion kept out of them, and only reverence for her there. And even at that the fugitive scarlet had stained the pale skin, and the eyes had widened and darkened upon me, asking, Tell me, explain what this mysterious feeling is that seems stirring faintly in me? And I had looked back at her in silence, with a word unuttered, but still perhaps divined by her, on my lips.

Later!

And now things had come to a crisis. I felt as if I could not stand any longer, clear-headed and hard-working as I had been, against this repeated raising, then deferring, then breaking down of hope.

Constantly I had given rein to my thoughts and wishes; many times I had said, "This book will certainly be accepted, and then a month or a few weeks and she is my own."

But the book had not been taken, the weeks passed by and Lucia was as far from me as ever. And it could not continue. The perpetual excitation and reaction was slowly injuring and confusing the brain like a noxious drug administered to procure lunacy. And the temptation swept over me now to let go my hold on work, on this bitter effort to succeed, on this vain, useless striving for recognition, and sink into some humble position which would supply the necessities for a quiet obscure existence - shared with this woman. The weeks, months, years, passed now, wasted, in a dull torture, in a low fever, filled with long, dragging hopes, expectations, possibilities, and no realities. Better sweep all these away and settle into a level, solid existence, contented with the simple natural pleasures that life offers without striving for. Contented! I laughed as the word drifted across my brain. That was just what I felt I could not be in any life but the one I coveted - a life of power, recognition, distinction. Other men were. They married the women they loved, and dropped into quiet lives of daily work and regular incomes, and were content in them. Yes; but that was insufficient argument.

They had not within them the suffocating weight of a desire ungratified, the stifling sense of a power unused. Nature, who has appointed no greater joy for us than the exercise of the capacities she has given us, has also no heavier, bitterer burden she can lay upon us than these capacities barred down in us unemployed. As I thought, my father's words recurred to me, "A secretary, a clerk or a shoeblack." It was improbable I should descend to the shoeblack. It was possible that I could become a secretary or a clerk. A secretary or a clerk! The idea amused me. I leaned my elbows on my knees, my forehead on my hands, as I sat and stared down at the bear-skin rug at my feet and saw a vision of fifth-rate existence pass before me. A suburban villa or squalid London lodgings; the hurried early breakfast served by a slavey; the tram or bus to the city; the society of seedy clerks; the pipe instead of the cigar; the public billiard room instead of the club; the omnibus instead of the hansom; the fortnight up the Thames instead of the spring at Cairo. A day of uncongenial work - but at the end of it Lucia!

The thought seemed to come suddenly and stunningly through my brain like a bullet. The blood rushed to my face and I got up and crossed to the window, looking out and seeing nothing. Lucia daily, hourly, side by side with me in my life, and utterly my own possession! Yes, it was worth it! Worth all those petty considerations that had been passing before me, but there was another heavier than all the others massed together. My leisure would be taken from me. It would be impossible to write then as I was writing now. Now, I was absolutely my own master, and disposed of my time exactly as I pleased, and days passed constantly which were wholly spent in the preparation of a manuscript and when my train of thought was never interrupted. If all my days were given to monotonous business work, how then, and when, would the writing be accomplished? My evenings and nights would be my own - or Lucia's; and this line of reflection finished in an ironical laugh. I walked to and fro, one word hammering persistently on my brain-sacrifice. To accept a humble, working position, and in it to marry a woman as lovely, as vehemently desired, and as long waited for as Lucia, would mean the sacrifice of my talent. It would mean a suppression, a thrusting aside of work, and, to a certain extent, of thought. In such a life there would be so little place for it. Between the necessity of rejecting impersonal or imaginative thought to make room for the diurnal business routine, and the irresistible temptations to reject it at other times for present personal pleasure, it would be rarely accepted or welcomed, and its impetus would gradually weaken or lessen. Even as I thought of it, a revolt rose in me. The revolt of all the higher instincts against enslavement by the lower. The rebellion of all the intellectual impulses against being ruled by the physical. What! weaken, enervate, starve, destroy the mental sinews to gratify the passion for a woman? Crush down the mental emotions to give reins to the physical? It would be the work of a fool. A rooting-up fruit trees to clear a space for weeds. And what of those twenty-six years of life that lay behind me? Did they count for nothing? Was all the repression and the hard work they contained to be flung aside now and wasted? Was the whole principle that had shaped them, of living in and for the intellect, to be utterly reversed now? And yet it was a wretched, poor, burdensome thing, life, as it had been lived by me. The past years stared me in the face mockingly. Clean, capable of being scrutinised in the sunlight, estimable from a moral and mental standpoint, but absolutely barren of pleasure, and, so far, barren of result. I looked at them with little satisfaction or pride. They were as immaculate, as bare, as denuded, as irritating, and as painful to contemplate as a chalk cliff. The character that is summed up in the line "video meliora proboque, detiora sequor" is supposed to be very common, and meets with universal comprehension and commiseration. Mine, perhaps, would find neither. I followed the good - that is, good as the world's opinion goes - the straight line in life, without any of the enthusiasm for virtue to form a consolation and support. I looked upon vice without that repulsion that makes resistance to it easy, pleasant, involuntary almost. I felt no sense of strong condemnation of those acts or failings or lapses in others which I studiously avoided myself. Therefore, I had neither the pleasure that might be derived from the evil itself, nor the warm satisfaction and personal pride that comes from conscious superiority to one's neighbours. I had lived the life of a Puritan, but I had neither the heart nor brain of one. None of the rigid bigotry, none of the exultant delight in morality, none of the merciless joy in trampling upon pleasure which gives him his reward. I looked round upon life and its many devious ways with eyes listless and indifferent to its vice and sympathetic to its pleasure, and back upon my own straight path with something of regret that my self-respect had been strong enough to hold me to it. And now the temptation came to sacrifice all that I had clung to. To abolish the thought and remembrance of my talent, muffle and stifle the powers of the brain, and remember only that I had the pulses and senses and blood of a man. It came over me slowly, this phase of rebellious animalism, like a mantle falling over me. Thought followed thought insidiously, imperceptibly, like fold upon fold of a cloth dropped upon me, as I sat in the silent room alone. To take this girl and force back her art upon itself, to mutilate her brain-power and drug it with her roused sensuality, to turn her into a simple instrument of pleasure for myself, and lend myself to her as such. To yield to this inflowing tide of desire that beat, now, heavily through all my veins, and let the brain go down beneath its waves.

If I chose I could do it, and none but myself could gauge the depth of my debasement. No eye could discern the high level ground now on which I stood and the morass that swam before me. I should marry this girl and the world asks no more. This other lower life that lay in my power appealed to me in all its sweetness - this woman as she would be when mine. Those lips with the mark of mine upon them; those delicate nerves stung to frenzy; that form tense, and the limbs strung with passion; those eyes terror-stricken between anguish and ecstasy.

The thought of the woman's personality clung to me like a viscous web. I struggled against it, but it enwrapped me; I could not shake it from me.

Again and again my arm encircled those soft yielding shoulders; the warm agitated bosom was touching mine; my hands held, and felt within it, the smooth muscles of the white arm - a vision of the whole indefinably supple form swam giddily before me in a suffocating proximity, till I pressed my hands on my eyes, and the thought came involuntarily, - Is this insanity?

My brain gave her into my arms now as I sat there, and the blind physical system clamoured in agony, Where is she? An hour passed, and then I got up and laughed. The destructive wave of emotion had risen in me, rolled through me and gone by. The struggle was over, and I lived again but to work. I stood on the rug rolling a cigarette, and lighted it leisurely, trying to recall a respectable calm, and when I had fairly succeeded I went out and downstairs. I came into the dining-room and found my father still there, looking through a budget of political pamphlets that had just come in by the post.

He looked up, and I met his eyes with a laugh.

"I have decided not to look out for a vacancy in the shoeblack line," I said; "but to go on - up the hill. Is there any claret or water or soda about - I don't much care what it is?"

"There is claret and soda too - there on the cheffonier. What a pity it is, Victor, you are so unreasonable! You make yourself look deplorably ill about every trifle! You are certainly trying to find a short cut out of the world! Why don't you take things more easily?"

"I am as I am," I muttered. "I'm going out now," I said, when I had finished the soda.

"I'm going to look Howard up. I have got a new plan of work if he'll join me in it. I shall see."

My father elevated his shoulders as much as to say, Some new phase of dementia, I suppose, and I went out.

I took the underground to Baker Street, and thence two minutes' walk brought me to the house I wanted. Howard was a friend of mine, an intimate friend, though, strictly speaking, from his character he ought not to have been.

As a general rule I steer clear of friendships with men who are very much opposed to me in character; it saves a lot of bother in the end. However, in this case, although I believed Howard to be a weak, worthless, untrustworthy individual, I could not help liking him. He was talented and of a pleasing - at least to me - personality. When I came into his room he was sitting reading in a long chair by the fire.

"Oh! is that you, Vic? Come in," he said, turning a good-looking discontented face towards me, not improved just now by the effects of a severe attack of jaundice.

"How are you?" I said, shaking his saffron-hued hand.

"Pretty beastly. And you?"

"Your remark might serve, I think," I said, taking a chair opposite him.

"Aren't you any better?" and I scanned his face closely.

He was not more than twenty, and had a singularly fine type of countenance.

"Oh yes, thanks! Crawling on."

"Any news?"

"None, I think, except that I've broken with Kitty."

I laughed.

"I knew you'd have to!" I said. "Did I not say so from the first? I felt sure you could never stand her!"

"I am rather sorry, for she was very pretty; but the last straw she put upon me was too much. I couldn't - after that - no, I couldn't, really."

"What was it?" I said, laughing, as he shook his head dubiously and looked meditatively into the fire.

"Why, I sent her a sonnet - at least, no, a verse - and we were talking about it afterwards, I had written -"

'And leaning sideways, looks, and lifts
The tresses of her heavy hair.'

"See?"

I nodded.

"Well, she objected to the adjective 'heavy,' and wanted me to insert another. What word do you think she suggested?"

"Can't say at all. Golden, perhaps!"

"Worse!" he answered, with a groan. "Golden is hackneyed but still conceivable. No - Crimpy! my dear fellow! Think of it!"

I went into a fit of laughter.

"Heavens! well I must say I never should have thought of that," I said. "What a fearful girl. And what did you say?"

"Say! I tried to explain to her the awfulness of it, the incongruity, but no, she couldn't see it! We jawed about it for a couple of hours with the result that our engagement is now off!"

"Good. I am very glad to hear it; but perhaps a Breach of Promise will come on?"

"Can't help it. Anything would be better than to go through life with a girl who didn't feel there are some things no fellar can do; and one of them, that he can't put a word like crimpy in his sonnet."

"Been doing any work?"

"Yes; one poem. Like to see it?"

"Very much."

He got up and went to a table littered all over with papers - written, printed, and blank. After a time he extracted the one he wanted, handed it to me, and then flung himself into the chair again.

"Whew! This title won't do. 'The Hermaphrodite!' That's far too alarming for the British public."

"Oh, bother! Well, go on. Read the poem."

I did so in silence.

"First-rate," I said, when I had finished. "Not a weak line in it. Not a single weak line. And there's nothing to prevent its being taken even in this d - d England, I think. The title's the worst part. You'll have to alter that."

"Why? Swinburne has a poem, 'Hermaphroditus.'"

"Yes - in a volume; and there it's Latinised; and then Swinburne has made his name, which of course is everything. If you want to make your debut before the English reading world you must do so with 'Ode to my father's tombstone,' or something of that sort!"

"Well, if you think Latin would improve it, let's put 'Duplexus' as its title," he answered, laughing and trying to snatch back the paper.

"Not on any account!" I said. "That would sound cynical, and cynical when you're unknown you must not be."

"Oh, well, there! I leave it to you to find a title! I don't care what it's called."

I looked through the verses trying to catch an idea for a name. Numbers suggested themselves to me, but none sufficiently vague and indefinite to suit the English ear. At last I said -

"Do you think Linked Spheres would do?"

"Linked Spheres?" replied Howard, with elevated brows. "What on earth has that to do with the subject?"

"Well, I have taken it from this line where you say, 'And in his brain are two divided worlds of thought.'"

"But I say that they are divided - divided isn't linked!"

"No, I quite admit it. But though divided they must be linked to a certain extent by being both within his brain. It is not quite right though, because the walls of the skull might, by encircling the two worlds, be said to unite them, but they could not 'link' anything. I follow all that, and I don't think the title is particularly artistic. It's not clear enough. Your own is much better from the view of intrinsic fitness. But the beauty of Linked Spheres is its indistinctness. You must not be too clear. That has been my great fault - perspicuity - and I am beginning to see it now. It has fatally barred my getting on. I always do try to make people see exactly what I mean, and that is apparently a mistake. When I write about passion everybody feels it is passion, and is shocked in consequence. When another fellow writes about it you feel he is trying to say something, but you are not quite sure what, and so it doesn't matter."

"'Muddle it! muddle it!' must be your watchword if you want to pass muster through the British press. Linked Spheres is a splendid muddle - very indefinite, quite void of connection with the subject in hand, and with a pleasant tinkle about the sound, just like Gladstone's speeches! Linked Spheres! It's impossible, for how the deuce would you link a sphere? Metaphor all wrong, and no one will know in the least what you mean, but it sounds pleasant and polished, and perfectly proper, and you'll find your editor will swallow the poem at a gulp."

Howard laughed.

"You're in an awful huff, Victor, with the British press, that's clear!"

I laughed too.

"Yes I am, I admit it, and all this leads up to the question I came to ask you this afternoon. Will you come over to Paris with me? I am going."

I got up and leant against the mantel-piece, pushing a place clear for my elbow on it between a bottle of liqueur and a copy of "The Holy Grail."

"You're great at springing mines upon one. Paris? why Paris? And how can you tear yourself away from Lucia?"

"I wish you would not pronounce that word as if it rhymed with Fuchsia," I said.

"Well, how do you want me to pronounce it?"

"You know quite well its Lu-chee-ah, and the accent is on the middle syllable, not the first."

"Oh, all right: Lu-CHEE-ah. Ah! what a mouthful! I would rather say Miss Grant!"

"It might be as well if you did," I said, coldly.

Howard looked at me and opened his eyes.

"You are uncommonly sticky to-day," he said, kicking a very old slipper off his swinging foot and catching it on the toe again.

"Well, what about Paris? Let's hear."

"I am so sick of this rotten, wishy-washy England. They won't take my things as they stand, and I'm not going to write 'Tales of my First Feeding Bottle' to please them. So I'm going over to Paris. I shall turn my MSS. into French and publish them there. The language lends itself to perfect lucidity, and the Paris press allows men to write as men. Besides, the French admire word-painting, which is my particular vein. The English don't. They like composition. Here an author's pen must remain always a stick dipped in ink. It must never become what mine is - a painter's brush, wet, dripping, over-flowing with oil colour. It struck me you might care to come too, and do the same with your verse. If so - come, by all means."

I looked down at his intelligent face and hoped he would come. Selfish, conceited, and self-sufficient as I may be, there is a strand of weakness made up in my composition that forces me to find the companionship of another intellect whenever possible.

"Yes; I'll come," he answered after a minute, getting on to his feet and thrusting both hands into his pockets with an energetic air. "I'm rather dubious about the books and the translation business; but anyway we can have a high old time in Paris!"

"But look here, Howard," I returned, "whether I succeed or not, I am not meditating having any high old time, or rather what you mean - a low old time. I'm going there to work."

"Oh, we all know you're a saint!" he said derisively. "But - 'A doubtful throne is ice on summer seas!' We shall see how long your virtue lasts at La Scala and in the Champs Elysees, with Lucia safely packed away in England!"

I smiled and raised my eyebrows in silence. The point was not worth discussing. Howard and I looked at some things from such an enormously different level that conversation on them was merely waste of time. It was as if a man upon a cliff started a dissertation with another in a boat lying on the sea beneath. Half the excellent arguments would drift away upon the wind, lost, rendered nil by the mere difference of level in the two planes. The two main chains that bound my whole psychological system - self-control and self-respect - were entirely absent in him. He looked at his every good action from the point of utility, at his every bad one from the point of secrecy. He would do the first if it were useful to him, and the last if it were secret. These, I believe, were the only two conditions that ever occurred to him. He was weak, even contemptible, in character, and I could not help clearly seeing it, but my friendship to him was won over by his talents, and by a certain good-tempered, easy, pleasant way he had. Widely different though we were, we had never had a quarrel. We got on together perfectly, and he might say things to me that would have offended me from an other man. Liking! Liking! What is it? It is as difficult to define, as impossible to imprison between the limits of motives and reasons, of "Whys" and "becauses," as Loving. I liked Howard, or rather I liked his society, which is not the same thing. Often the people who are the most disappointing in the great issues of life are the pleasantest to live with through the trifles of everyday existence and vice versa. I would not have trusted Howard in a crisis for any consideration, but then crises don't come every day, and he was delightful to discuss a chapter or a sonnet with.

"When are you going, by the way? Not to-morrow, I hope, for behold this room!" and he glanced round helplessly.

It was certainly in the most frightful of literary confusions. Masses of loose papers, letters, bills, poems, drifted over the tables; books stood in piles upon the floor; newspapers occupied the chairs.

"No, next week. Shall we say Saturday?"

"All right. I'll be ready by then. Cross - evening, I suppose?"

"Very likely. But I shall see you again," I said, looking at my watch. "By Jove! close to seven. I must go. Try and get rid of that confounded jaundice. Good-bye!"

Howard extended his hand.

"By the way, what about the tin? Can you manage?" -

"Oh yes! That's all right," I said.

I was Howard's bank, upon which he drew fitfully and spasmodically: that is to say, when any expensive little fancy seized him. He always insisted on giving me I.O.U.'s and acknowledgments for the sums he borrowed, which I as regularly tore in pieces and put in the fire. I was half way down the stairs when I ran back and opened his door again.

"Howard!"

"Hullo!"

"Have you a copy of that verse? I have not half studied it this evening."

"What?" he said, looking round his chair back. "Your precious Linked Spheres? Yes; take that one if you like."

I took up the paper.

"Thanks!" I said, and re-descended the stairs.

Going down Baker Street, I stopped at the first lamp-post, and read some lines of it again. A glow of admiration, almost of affection, towards the curious lines, full of nascent genius, lit slowly in me.

"Splendid! magnificent!" I muttered. "If not here, I'll see it's got out in Paris."

CHAPTER III

The next week saw myself and Howard installed in Paris. We had two large, comfortable rooms on the second floor, opening into each other, well furnished and upholstered in every way as sitting-rooms, as most of the French bedrooms are.

They faced a corner where several boulevards met and diverged, and there was a constant stream of Paris life flowing beneath our windows every hour of the day. A balcony ran outside, and on this in the evening we used to stand and smoke and flick paper balls on to the heads of the grisettes and the bonnes passing far underneath. On the ground floor of the hotel was a cafe that extended also over the pavement with its chairs and tables, and was open to the general public as well as to those who were staying in the hotel.

Howard and I got on admirably as usual. Although we were so different we had the common ground of a similarity in intellect. On all strictly intellectual subjects, in psychological discussions, on points of artistic merit, we seldom differed. His brain was, when he chose to exert it, singularly brilliant, and in a companion this compensates me for everything else almost that is wanting. I could not certainly have lived in the same intimacy with a fool who had been as high principled, as moral, and as sober as Howard was the reverse of all these. Our mode of life was very different, as naturally it would be, since I had come with a predetermination to do nothing but work, and he with an equally strong one to idle his days away in the most enjoyable manner he could invent. For myself, I was fairly content with the prospect before me. Work I was accustomed to, and it was easy. A new idea for a manuscript had begun to hover fitfully before my mental vision, and was gradually absorbing my thoughts into itself. Had I been able to write to and hear from Lucia I should have been satisfied, but my father had made the absence of all correspondence between us a sine qua non of my coming here. When I had heard this I had looked at him with some little amusement. Such a stipulation as this seemed to me to have only one interpretation - he hoped and thought I should forget her!

"What is the meaning of this?" I asked. "What can be the benefit of it? How can the fact of our writing or not writing be of importance? Do you think I shall ever relinquish Lucia? I am resigned to wait as long as must be, but I am utterly determined to have her in the end."

To which my father had answered grimly with a smile, -

"Very well, my dear Victor, see that you get her!"

Which remark had made me grind my teeth and then laugh and shrug my shoulders.

"And you won't permit a letter a month?"

"No."

"Oh, dressed in your little brief authority!" I thought, looking at him. Then I said -

"Very good - I agree."

"I consider I have your word that you will not write, nor hear from her, directly or indirectly, within this year?"

"Certainly you have."

And so the matter was settled.

When Lucia heard of it, we met each other's eyes, and she elevated her eyebrows, and a faint smile curved her lips.

"It will make no difference," she murmured, and nothing more.

After all, I don't know that I cared very greatly about the letters. It was Lucia herself that I wanted - nothing less. It gives me very little pleasure to read a letter, and I never have understood the cherishing locks of hair and dead roses business.

The desire for the presence of the living personality is too sharp-edged to let me feel satisfaction in substitutory objects and vague associations. To have put my hand round Lucia's living throat; yes, that would have been a keen delight, but I was not dead set on possessing myself of her handkerchief that I might kiss in private. I had one portrait of her - that was all - and that I rarely looked at.

The first thing I did in Paris was to find a translator for Howard's poem, which, after a time, appeared in one of the literary papers in its French dress, and returned to its original title. He came to me suddenly one evening with a contemporary paper in his hand, and the flush of gratified talent, and the pride that is its first cousin, kindling in his face.

"Look here, Vic!" he said; "isn't this first-class? Here's a critique on my verses, and just see how they crack them up!"

I took the paper and read the paragraph, Howard leaning over my shoulder and resting his knee on the arm of my chair. When I had finished I looked up at him.

"Not a word more than it deserves, old man!" I said. "Now you realise, don't you, what you can be and do if you choose!"

"Yes. Well, really, if all that's true, I ought to make some sort of a name some day, eh?"

And for a time it seemed that a lasting impression had been made upon him. He seemed to feel that elation and enthusiasm stir in him which makes it a joy to the genius to renounce all for his work. With regard to my own manuscripts, I sent some of them, in English, to one of the French publishing firms, and there ensued a blank of three weeks. At the end of that time I received a peremptory note inviting me to call at their office. When I presented myself I was shown into a bare, square room, where an august little man was standing, using a silver toothpick. He was short, with a large-sized lower chest; bald, with a short, grey beard cut to a sharp point; waxed moustache ends, sticking out ferociously; and brown eyes, keen with intelligence. He bowed elaborately.

I could speak French, he supposed.

I assented, and the conversation then went on very fast.

Monsieur's works had been read by their Anglo-French reader and highly approved. There was no doubt that Monsieur possessed a talent, a talent that he would say was - colossal. At the same time, these works were all too English in tone to catch the taste of the Parisian world, and Monsieur had seemed to put a restraint upon his pen, that rendered his works a touch too cold.

Great heavens! how I raised my eyebrows at that; remembering that in England I had been always rejected on account of being too warm.

Now, his proposition was this: - If Monsieur felt disposed to write a manuscript, in which the scene should be laid in France, and some of the characters, at least, be French, and also allow himself a little greater latitude, then he should be delighted to put the manuscript in the hands of their very best translator, and give it out to an audience that, above all things, admired vigour.

I heard all this with satisfaction. The offer meant a lot more work for me, but I did not mind that, with success - dear success - in view. I closed with his proposition at once, and after some formalities and details had been gone into and settled, I rushed home to tell Howard.

So, for a time, settled into working intellectual grooves, our life ran on quietly from day to day with a fair prospect on ahead of us.

And then came an unlucky incident which jerked the wheels of Howard's existence out of the narrow, hard line of effort, and after that they ran along anyhow, sometimes on and sometimes off it, and kept me in dread of a total smash. The Champs Elysees were full of the late afternoon sunlight, and we sauntered slowly, criticising the occupants of the various carriages rolling up to the great arch of Napoleon, and arguing in a broken, desultory way on our usual subject of talk - literature.

Howard was on the outside, nearest the road, walking on the actual kerb, and flicking up the leaves in the gutter, as he talked, with the point of his cane. As we strolled, with our eyes more or less directed on the string of vehicles moving in the centre of the sunny road, we noticed one small, black brougham going the same way as ourselves, that seemed conspicuous by being closed amongst the rest of the open victorias. Suddenly it detached itself from the line of other carriages and dashed up alongside of the pavement where we were walking. Its wheels ground in the gutter, and I caught Howard's arm to draw him more on to the pavement.

"Look out!" I exclaimed. "What a way to drive!" I added, as the coachman whipped up his horses and drove on some fifty yards, close to the kerb. There he pulled up abruptly. The door of the brougham was pushed open and a woman got out. Such a figure it was that outlined itself in the sunny light, standing on the white trottoir, and with the vista of the Champs Elysees behind it - a form seductive in every line, with a fine hip, and a tiny arched foot that tapped the pavement impatiently.

"What's up?" I said to Howard. "Whom is she waiting for, I wonder?"

A few steps more brought us up to her, and then, to our astonishment, she turned fully towards me, and said in her own language, -

"Will you come and dine with me this evening, Monsieur? The carriage will take us home now!"

We both stopped short. There was a second of blank amaze, and the woman's face stamped itself on our startled vision; - the eyes, liquid and gleaming, behind a veil of black lashes; the smooth firm nose, with its raised and tremulous nostril; the oval of either cheek, with the damask glow in it; and the curled mouth of deepest crimson, with the essence of sensuous languor in its curve.

For a second we stared at it in the sunlight, and that second sufficed to let us take in the situation; and there was something in her words and tone of confidence, and something of authority in the way she pointed to her carriage, that annoyed me.

"Thank you! I only dine with my friends," I answered coldly.

I suppose she was not insensible to the contempt in my tone and eyes as I looked down on her, for her next words came in a more humble, ingratiating voice.

"Make me one of them, then, Monsieur! - at once;" and she smiled - a lovely smile on such a mouth. Howard stood in silence, staring at her. I was very much amused and a little annoyed.

"You flatter me!" I returned, satirically; "but I have as many as I want already."

Howard broke in.

"Won't you extend your invitation to me?" he said, eagerly, and she threw a quick side-glance over him.

"I can't invite you both - at the same time!" she said, with a laugh and a little Parisian shrug; and then she looked at me again with a look that one would say was abominable or charming, according as one's particular mood at the moment was.

My mood was not such as to condemn it.

My next words were simply said for me, as it were, by my long habit of self-restraint.

"My presence is not in the question at all, to embarrass you," I said, curtly, and added to Howard -

"We may as well go on."

But that was not at all his view.

"Ask me," he said, with his shaky French accent; "I'll come!" and he put his hand on her arm, with a glance that matched her own. She seemed pretty well indifferent which of us it should be, and she merely said imperiously, -

"Come, then!" and with a grimace over her shoulder at me, disappeared into her brougham again.

Howard would have followed instantly, but I seized his arm.

"What are you doing?" I said in English. "Is it worth it, Howard? You may regret it. She is probably some married woman!"

Howard wrenched himself free from me.

"Don't talk to me! I'm not the fellow to refuse a jolly good lark when it's offered to me!"

He flung himself into the brougham without another word, drew the door to after him, and they were gone, whirling up the Champs Elysees, leaving me standing on the kerb looking after the polished black back of the brougham receding and growing small in the distance.

"Well!" I thought, "if another fellow had told me this tale, I should have thought it a howler!"

The suddenness of the whole thing had taken my breath away, and I must have stood there many seconds in confused thought, in which a flexible form and arched foot took a prominent part.

When I roused myself I saw Nous was lying down beside me with the patience of a philosopher, and catching the flies that buzzed along the sunny pavement - to kill time.

I called him, and went on up toward the Arc.

"I couldn't have done otherwise," I thought. I knew I did not wish to have done otherwise. I knew I should say again exactly the same if the brougham were again before me, but yet -

"I want nothing now that I have my work on hand," I told myself, as the arched foot went on before me up the pavement.

"By-and-by" - but then life seemed all by-and-bys for me.

I shortened my walk. Everything seemed to jar upon my nerves. I went back to the hotel by a quiet way, and then up to the empty room to work.

Howard did not return for a couple of days. On the third I was sitting after dinner at one of the tables outside the hotel cafe, smoking, under the line of trees that edge the Paris kerb, when a fiacre drew up at my very elbow, and Howard got out. He did not see me for a minute, engaged with paying the cocher and hunting for a pourboire, and then he was just going straight across the lighted trottoir into the hotel when I called to him.

"Hullo, Vic! there you are!" he said, turning back. "I didn't see you under the tree."

He came back and drew up a chair, with a scraping sound, to the opposite side of my table, leant his elbows upon it, and pushed his hat back. There was a blaze of light, all across the pavement to where we were sitting, from the windows and open glass doors of the cafe. He looked well and uncommonly jolly; a man who lives his life, such as it is, without thought, without reflection, and without philosophy - who views the passing hour without grudging, the past without regret.

"You look awfully seedy," he said. "Anything up?"

"No," I answered. "Well? 'How have we sped in this contest?' How went the dinner?"

"I'll tell you," he said, turning round to secure a passing garcon. "Let's get hold of a drink first. Oh, she's got a jolly place!" he said, when the garcon, and eventually the drink, had been captured. "Nice house and all that. She's married, as you said, and of very good family. Received everywhere, you know."

"Husband at the dinner?" I asked laconically.

"No; husband gone to Tunis on business."

"Expected back to-day, I suppose?"

"No, to-morrow."

"Pity."

"Yes. You should have gone, Vic! She'd have satisfied you! Lovely figure! I never knew a lovelier!"

I said nothing.

"What did you think of her stopping us like that?" he went on after a minute.

"I thought it consummate cheek," I said. "I should not have believed it if it hadn't actually happened before my eyes."

"Yes, it was cheeky; but do you know, she is not very cheeky, really. An awfully nice woman, and very clever. But aren't these Parisiennes queer? You can't imagine any woman doing such a thing in England, can you?"

"Hardly."

"It seems she had seen us once before. It was you she wanted, not me. Why didn't you go, you duffer? I only came in a bad second!"

I laughed.

"She had read my things and likes them. Do you know, I think it is rather a good thing I have met her, it will urge me to do more - don't look at me 'in that tone of voice,' I am sure it will, really, Victor!"

"Are you going to see her again, then?" I asked.

"Yes, oh yes!"

"When the husband next visits Tunis, I suppose?"

"Yes, and before that, even when he's here. She is going to patronise my talent - see?"

"I see."

"I must write my next thing to her, of course. It's a nuisance being hampered with this beastly French language!"

And then the conversation went on. We sat there and talked and argued from the particular to the general, and back again, until the waiters came and cleared the chairs off the pavement and began to turn out the lights in the cafe - and it was a conversation after which I slept badly.

After this incident I saw less of Howard, and our lives ran farther and farther apart. I grew more and more absorbed in the developing manuscript. He grew more and more taken up in the stream of amusement he had entered. He wrote very little. A couple of lines that had occurred to him perhaps at the theatre, and were jotted hastily on the edge of a programme, was all that a whole week produced. And even these would have been lost through his carelessness but for me.

The days were generally divided between headache and sleep; the nights between the theatre and drink. I regretted it; and this life that was being wasted, poured out in uselessness, within my sight oppressed me. I should hardly have noticed it with another man, but I knew that this one had been planned for higher things.

I used to try and rouse in him his pride and love for himself, or, at any rate, for his talent. I used to insist on his hearing me read sometimes those disconnected lines that his own brain, dulled by drink, had almost forgotten.

"Are they not splendid?" I would say; "and you are the author! You are their parent, Howard! Think! Any man could lead the life you are leading! not one in a thousand could produce these lines!"

Howard would look at me suspiciously with heavy eyes.

"Are you sure I wrote that? I don't think I remember it!"

What a crime!

"I know you did," I would answer, and then urge him to give

every day and night in the week, if he liked, to pleasure except one - "let one be sacred to work!"

"And just think," he would answer, lazily, "if I were dying, how those days and nights wasted would come and stare me in the face!"

"Wasted! in the building of such lines as these?"

"But what's the good of them when they are built? They don't make me enjoy life!"

And he pursued his own path and I could not stop him. I hoped and thought he would get tired after a time of the Paris halls and drunken nights and sick headaches, but I waited in vain. He had gradually got intimate with the back as well as the front of the scenes, and this I liked less than anything. The state of Howard's finances, too, threw an extra weight of responsibility on me, for he must have trodden a straighter road, and perhaps he would have worked more if he had had less money. And the money - his superfluous cash - came generally from me. His own allowance was small; just enough to keep him and no more. Gifts, under the name of loans, from me supplied all extras, and filled all deficiencies and gaps. What could I answer when he used to say, "Dear old boy! let me have another twenty!" And yet I knew it was handing him the razor to cut his throat. I hoped the sight of another fellow working as persistently as I did would have been an encouragement to him to make some sort of effort himself, but he looked upon me as a misguided creature, and took pains not to follow my example.

"How do you know that you will ever marry Lucia? or make a success of your books or anything?" he asked me one evening as we went upstairs after dinner, he to dress before going to La Scarletta, I to work on the MS.

"You are working for an uncertainty, a dream. It may never come off, and then where will you be. Now, at least, I know what I am going to have this evening. Such enjoyment as there is I get it, and there's an end of it, and no worry about it. As for you, you are all worry; and even granted that you get, in the end, something superlatively satisfactory, why, it will hardly make up to you for all you have gone through to get it!"

I said nothing. We had got up to our rooms by this time, and I flung myself into the easy chair.

Howard went into his room and brought back his dress shoes to put them on in mine, that he might follow up his argument.

"Now, look here, Vic, which of us two fellows is the most ready to go out of the world? In the Bible or prayer-book or somewhere we are told to live so that we may be willing and prepared to die any minute. Well, that's just what I do. I haven't a scrap of a tie to life. I don't think there will be anything better in it than what I have had already. I'd go tomorrow. But you, you would not like it a bit, and you can't deny it. You have got all the ties of your unsatisfied desires. You want to get Lucia - you want to make your name. You would be awfully cut up now if you were told you were going to be bundled out of life in ten minutes; and I - I shouldn't care!"

Howard had finished fastening his patent shoes, and now sat back in his chair, one leg crossed over the other, and his hands behind his head.

"Being brought into life is just like being invited to a feast from which you may be called away at any minute. Well, if you have eaten and drunk to satiety you will be only too glad to get up and go away and sleep. But if you have sat at the table, hungering all the time and repressing yourself, then, when the sudden call comes, and you must rise and leave it for ever, think what a misery and bitterness to be dragged away from the brilliant table, with all its dishes and its wines untasted, its flowers unsmelt, and be crammed away into the darkness - hungry, thirsty, and unsatisfied. Take my word for it, Vic, you'll have a bad five minutes on your deathbed!"

I listened in silence. I felt ill and dispirited and disinclined for talk.

"That's all Horace. I don't care much about Latin as a whole, but I do think he is splendid. I'd have that book made the general testament. I'd have it taught in all the Board Schools and sworn on in the Law Courts. I'd have every fellow take it as a guide through life; if he really acts up to it, it ensures his happiness. Its philosophy beats all the religions hollow. ' Take the day.' 'Put no trust in to-morrow.' ' Seek not to know the future; whatever it is, bear it.' 'Each night be able to say I have lived.' 'Retire from life, satisfied, as from a banquet.' And so on ad lib. You know it all, Victor. You were brought up upon it, but you haven't profited by it - not a scrap. Well, I'm going!"

He leant forward, picked up his shoes, and went into his own room. It was about twelve when he came in that night and found me just finishing off a chapter. The fire had gone out from neglect; the window stood open and the lace curtains waved in the damp night wind. Howard stalked across the room and banged the glass doors shut, and told me it was beastly cold in here. I was just fully absorbed in the closing passages of my scene, and felt a nervous irritation at being interrupted.

"There's a fire-lighter behind the scuttle, throw it into the grate and you'll soon have a blaze," I said, without looking up.

Howard drew off his lavender gloves and flung them down on the table. One fell on the last sheet I had written.

"Confound you! do be careful!" I muttered, picking it up, and noticing the great blur it left on the page. "The sheets are wet."

"It doesn't matter, they're not a new pair!" answered Howard, coolly, going down on his knees to light up the fire. He accomplished this in a few minutes, and then settled down in the long chair with a cigar. I wrote on feverishly, expecting to be addressed and interrupted every moment. It was a great bore his coming in just now, disturbing me. I had a difficult thing to express, and I was just pursuing the tail end of an idea I could not quite grasp. My pen hovered uncertainly over the paper. I could not exactly give words to the impression in my brain, and the sense that he was going to speak, about to speak each second, worried me. At the same time I never wished to be ungracious to Howard when he did return to our rooms; never wished to feel it was my execrably bad company that induced him to stay away from them all night instead of half.

"I say, Vic!"

"Well?"

"Do you know that kissing song Embrasse moi?"

I nodded.

"Don't you think it awfully fetching? I like that refrain so much - Embrasse moi, chumph! chumph! - and then the orchestra exactly imitates the sound of a kiss - then Encore une fois!! chumph! chumph! Don't you?"

"Yes; it isn't bad."

Silence.

"Victor!"

"What?"

"La Faina was there to-night!"

"Oh!"

"Do you know her?"

"I've heard of her."

Silence.

"Vic!"

"Yes?"

"Do you know what Faina means?"

"Of course I do!"

"Do you think it a nice name?"

"Not particularly."

"Well, it's better than Grille d'Egout anyway, isn't it?"

"About on a par, I should say." "How many frills do you think she had on her petticoat?"

"Oh, I don't know - forty!"

"No; four. I counted them. Her figure is not much up atop, but her" -

"Oh, stow all that!" I interrupted; "there's a good fellow, I'm just doing a convent interior."

"All right. The rest is silence. Ah!" with a yawn, and getting up to saunter round the room, "that's a jolly good song - Embrace moi! chumph! chumph! Encore une fois!! chumph! chumph!"

He did not address me again, but somehow my ideas were scattered. The convent scene went wrong. Ballet dancers seemed standing in the aisle where nuns should have been kneeling, and, after a second or so, I flung my pen down and pushed away the paper.

"Done?" exclaimed Howard, delightedly.

"Yes," I said simply, rising.

"Come and have a smoke," he said, drawing up both easy chairs to the fire.

I took the cigar he offered and sat down. Howard threw himself into the other chair, crossed his legs, and proceeded to give me an account of his experiences. I suppose I was rather silent, for after a time he broke in upon himself by saying abruptly, -

"Are you very savage with me for interrupting your work?"

"Savage?" I repeated. "Oh, no! the work can wait, I get plenty of time at it!" Perhaps he misunderstood me, and my words conveyed to him more than I meant. Any way, the next afternoon he came home early to dine with me, and afterwards, when I was speaking of the evening's work, he came up to me where I stood at the mantelpiece and took something out of his pocket with a confident air.

"I've brought you something," he said, and he thrust suddenly into my hand - under my eyes - a photograph.

My glance fell full on it, and I saw distinctly what it was - a full-length figure of the danseuse Faina. Traditionally, perhaps, I ought to have flung it into the fire - any way the grate - or torn it up. But I am not fond of throwing other, people's things into the fire, nor of tearing them up, simply because they offend my own views. He had no right, perhaps, to thrust it upon me as he had, but that fact would not, in my opinion, constitute my right to destroy it. So I merely laid it on the mantelpiece.

"Extraordinary thing! Where did you pick that up?"

"Faina sent it to you with her love, and an invitation to supper to-night after the last 'turn,'" replied Howard, rolling a cigarette, sticking it with his lips, and looking at me over it.

"Oh! really? "I said, drily.

"Why, Victor, you've quite coloured up!" said Howard with a sort of derisive triumph.

I felt I had. Why? I can hardly say. The word "love," the sudden view of the portrait, dashed, whirling headlong over each other, through my brain, followed by a sort of hazy cloud, out of which looked two azure eyes.

"She is very lovely, isn't she?" Howard remarked affectionately, setting the card upright against the wall.

"Very - in her own way," I assented.

I admitted it willingly, with pleasure. Why not? - an evident fact. The blue slime in a blocked gutter of the road is very lovely also.

"Well, I'm going there to-night, because I admire the sister, and you must come, too. You are killing yourself by sticking to the work in the way you do. Come along! Where's the harm? Lucia will never know. I won't split. God's in heaven and the Czar's a long way off! So you may as well come and knock about a little. This monotonous life will put an end to you!"

I was silent.

"Lucia won't know," he repeated.

"There's no question of Lucia's knowing anything," I said.

"Then why do you work as you do, and always refuse to come to a supper, or a dance, or anything? You can't be really a quiet fellow or you wouldn't write things the English won't have. You say it's not a question of Lucia - then what the dickens is it that makes you live the life you do?"

I did not answer him. I leant in silence against the mantelpiece, staring absently at the portrait of Faina, and Howard got tired of waiting for my answer. He went to dress, and I sat down at the writing-table, absently sketching women's heads on my blotting paper. Should I go with him or not? I felt tired of writing, tired of work. Wine, laughter, sound, smiles, other voices? - Then four points rose before me, very distinct and clear, like sharp mountain peaks from a valley of mist.

FIRST. Supposing - if such a thing were possible - supposing on coming out of this house I came face to face with Lucia, should I be entirely pleased.

NEXT. Should I, when the present inclination were over, have a satisfactory memory of this supper.

NEXT. Did I habitually mean to spend my evenings in this way?

LAST. Was it worth while spoiling a record for the sake of a single deviation?

I answered No to each of these as they came before me in order, with the upshot that I determined not to go. When Howard came in again I looked up. He was dressed to the Enth, and as I glanced at his good-looking, intelligent face, I thought how incongruous it seemed for him to degrade himself with drink at this supper, and return, as he probably would, a pitiable object to look at and listen to.

"Going to work, eh?"

I nodded. Howard hitched the cape of his overcoat straight, and went out. As he shut the door I sprang suddenly to my feet. For a moment the impulse towards distraction, amusement, relief from strain, physical movement, overcame me. All the strong, ardent life rushed up within me. A tremendous prompting came to shout after him, "Wait a minute, Howard! I'll come, too, after all!" I was half way to the door. Then I laughed and turned back. I went up to the mantelpiece and unlocked the doors of a portrait frame that stood there, and flung them open. It was the frame of Lucia's portrait, which, like the temple of Janus, stood closed in times of peace and open in times of war. Now was war, and I gazed at the picture within for encouragement. There was equal sinuous, supple beauty in this form as in that outline on the Paris card, that lay, perhaps, in the pocket of every flaneur on the boulevards. I looked at the smooth, perfect shoulders, and those soft arms that had never yet been drawn round a lover's neck; at the extreme pride and dignity that lay in every line of the form that had never been touched by a rough hand. It swept from me in one gust the thoughts and tendencies struggling to rise. It brought back all the old revolt from the lowest, all the old admiration for the highest, in human nature. "Yes, you are worth it," I muttered, looking hard at the chaste, exquisite pride in face and form; "you are worth being worthy of, and I will not for an evening, nor for an hour, make myself a brute that you would despise if you knew his nature. Whether you ever know or not, what does that matter? I must know. Shall I come back to feel your inferior? No! Not a day, nor a night, shall there be, the history of which you might not read." All my own pride was stirred as I looked at the portrait of this woman, who, I knew, was absolutely pure, and I would not now have followed Howard had my life depended on it.

I gave the photograph of Faina, which still stood up against the wall, a flick that sent it horizontal on the marble, and then, with Lucia's eyes just above me, I sat down to write.

Seven o'clock came, and the bright light pouring into the room over the table covered with loose sheets of paper found me writing still. I looked up, then back on the page, decided I need not add another word, flung down my pen, leaned back in my chair, and proceeded to light up a cigar. "Good!" I thought with lazy satisfaction, as my eyes wandered over the completely covered table and the drying sheets upon the floor.

"It was a splendid inspiration that! Had I gone out last night, infallibly I should have missed it." Just then I heard a blundering, uncertain step upon the stair, and then a dig in the centre of the door panel.

I smiled.

"How long will it take him to find the lock, I wonder?" I thought.

The period was protracted. Round and round the keyhole did a shaky, unsteady hand guide the wandering key. It scratched above, it dug at the door beneath, while the low indistinct murmur of one repeated word reached me within. At last, in sheer pity, I got up and opened the door from the inside. Howard came unsteadily over the threshold, and half blundered against me. His face was deadly pale; a bright greenish shade lay close about his bloodshot eyes; his grey lips shook. With difficulty he staggered to the chair opposite me and sat down. I shut the door and resumed my seat and cigar.

"Enjoy yourself?" I asked.

He was not very steady on his feet, but fairly clear in his brain.

"Yes. But it's no good - can't stand it," he murmured, pressing his hand hard upon his head and across his eyes.

His voice was little more than a gasp.

"God! - this weakness" -

We sat without speaking. In the bright light, in a glass opposite, I caught sight of my own face. I was as pale as he from work, as he from pleasure. My eyes were as bloodshot as his from sleeplessness, as his from drink. My hand shook as much as his from mental excitement, as his from physical exhaustion. He was the representative of those who sacrifice to-morrow for to-day. I, of those who sacrifice to-day for to-morrow. And I wondered, as I smoked on with his collapsed figure before me, which was the greater fool. "Do neither" is the cry. "Take the gifts of to-day without robbing to-morrow." Estimable rule, I agree, if you are fortunate enough to have the chance of carrying it out. But very few of us have. A man with Howard's constitution could only purchase the hours last night with the hours of this morning. Success would not come to me to-morrow unless I were willing to struggle for it to-day.

"What did you drink?" I asked, after a pause.

"Maraschino, cognac, and clic," he answered, and a gesture of his hand and first finger showed he meant in the same glass. I laughed.

"What a mixture! No wonder you're mixed yourself!"

"Can't stand it!" he only muttered again.

"No, you must sit it out or sleep it off now," I said, getting up with a stretch. "Faina in good form?"

"Magnificent - Vic, you should have been there!"

"Thanks! yes, I think so!" I said, gathering up the precious pages from the floor and table and piling them on a console. I wanted to go and get my own breakfast, but the look of Howard's face, as it lay against the chair back, bloodless, and the colour of ashes, made me hesitate to leave him.

"Can I get you anything?" I said.

"No - help me into bed," he muttered, without opening his eyes, moving his head restlessly from side to side.

"Come along, then," I answered, bending over him; "here's my arm."

He half raised his lids at that, and then feebly pushed a leaden hand and arm through mine. There was a pause. He seemed unable to make a farther movement, and sat, his head sunk into his chest, his arm hanging through mine.

"Come, Howard, make an effort," I said, after a minute, and he staggered uncertainly to his feet.

Getting him into the next room and into bed was a lengthy and difficult matter, but at last, after protracted pauses, it was effected, and he fell back upon the pillows - face and lips one tint with the linen. I spoke to him, but I got no articulate answer, only groans in response.

"I am going to fetch you some coffee," I said, leaning over him.

His eyes opened wide, and fixed upon me with a sort of helpless terror.

"No, no! don't go! - stay!" he whispered, clutching my wrist with his damp, shaking fingers. "Stay - a minute."

"But you want something to pull you round. I shan't be two seconds," I answered, trying to unclasp his clinging fingers.

"Never mind! Oh, Vic, for God's sake stay."

There was an abject appeal in the bloodshot eyes, a desperate tenacity in his clutch. He looked at me as if he dared look nowhere else. Some horror seemed pressing upon his confused and weakened brain, and I thought I could soothe him best by staying.

"Very well - there, I'm not going," I said, reassuringly.

Still he did not relax his grip upon me, but his eyes closed again, and he seemed satisfied. I sat down on a chair at the bedside and waited. The sun poured brighter and brighter through the blinds and touched up the mantelpiece.

The photograph of Faina's sister, surrounded by some others of her set, was propped up in the centre of it, on a couple of paper volumes. My own head was aching violently now, and after a time the woman's figure on the glossy, sun-flecked surface of the card began to sway and swim before my eyes as I looked lazily at it.

The minutes passed by and Howard did not move. At last, I ventured to try and withdraw my stiffening arm without rousing him, but at the first movement his fingers tightened and his groans recommenced.

After a time my hunger passed into drowsiness. I leant forward gradually, and at last my head sank down on the edge of his bed, and I drifted into oblivion.

CHAPTER IV

May had come round again. The days and weeks had glided by in a monotony of work, varied by feverish blanks when I could do nothing, and the pile of manuscript lay growing dusty in its corner. Then at last the day arrived when the final line was written and the whole despatched. That was three months back, three months of anxious waiting, in which Howard had chaffed me daily on my looks and health.

"You're dwindling to a most interesting skeleton, Vic," he used to say. "Catch me bothering myself about anything I wrote in the same way."

Now, however, it was over. I had just left the publisher's office. The book had been accepted, and I was a free man. A gush of fresh life ran through me and stirred in my veins in response to the fresh life of spring that seemed in the sunny air, in the green leaves fluttering round the Bourse, in the white butterflies that floated across the dusty asphalt.

When I got back I found Howard half asleep in the armchair. He sat up as I came in, and regarded me with a confused stare. I saw he had been drinking, but his brain was still tolerably clear.

"Rejected, by Jove!" he remarked as he saw the MS.

"No," I answered, throwing it on to a side table and myself into the chair opposite him - "no, thank heaven, it's all right now! They've accepted it. Congratulate me!"

"But what on earth have you brought it back for, then?" he said, blinking his heavy eyes and looking at me resentfully, as if he suspected I was playing some practical joke.

"Oh, there are a few things they want altered, that's all," I answered. "I am to let them have it again the day after to-morrow."

"And what about terms?" he continued, getting out a roll of cigarette papers and beginning to roll himself some cigarettes.

He was wide awake now, and had shaken off his intoxicated stupor. His face was bent slightly as he made the cigarettes, so that I could hardly see it. I sat watching his trembling fingers rolling the papers in an absent silence.

"Oh, terms?" I said at last. "Fairly good, I think. They pay me a small sum and reserve me one-third of all profits from the book. I really don't care much about the terms. Once the book is out my name is made, and the money will come in all right in time. They've taken it; that is the main point. If you knew the glorious relief it is to me!"

Howard laughed. He flung himself back in the chair and propped his feet up against the support of the mantelpiece.

"I think you are very lucky," he said. There was silence, then he asked abruptly - "How much are they going to give you for it?"

"Three thousand francs."

Howard paled suddenly and fixed his eyes upon me.

"And what will you do with it?" he asked, after a minute.

"Well," I answered, without reflection, "I thought you would like two thousand to send home and get rid of that half-yearly interest."

The blood dyed all his face suddenly crimson, and he brought down his feet upon the fender with a crash.

"I wish to hell you'd wait till I asked you for it!" he said savagely, springing up and crossing to the window.

There he stood looking out with his hands thrust deep into his pockets. I was fairly startled, and the colour rose uncomfortably in my own face.

It seemed, I almost felt, as if I had done something excessively ill-bred. But Howard and I were on such intimate terms, and made so little account of what we said to each other, that I had expressed the thought uppermost in my mind at the moment of his question as a matter of course. Then, too, he borrowed so constantly and so freely from me that the idea of offence over money matters or mentioning them seemed quite impossible.

"No," I thought, glancing at him as he still stood between me and the light; "there must be something else in his mind," and I wondered.

He was seldom out of temper, and seldom made himself disagreeable to me. In conversation, in all our life together, he generally yielded to me with an almost womanly compliance. His present tone and manner were absolutely new to me. I did not understand them, and I liked him well enough to take the trouble to get up after a second and follow him to the window.

"Howard," I said gently, "what is the matter? I am sorry if I have annoyed you."

He turned upon me suddenly from the window.

"Did I ever say I wanted the money you might get from your

cursed book?" he said, passionately. "Do you suppose I couldn't get as much for something of my own if I chose?"

Now, considering Howard was always in want of money, and perpetually lamenting his inability, real or imagined, to get it, the last remark seemed rather odd, and the vehemence with which he spoke against me was altogether incomprehensible.

"Of course," I answered quietly, looking down into his excited face. "I merely offered the money as a convenience, pro tem, as it happened to be at hand, that's all. But surely it doesn't matter. Perhaps I should not have done. I apologise. Doesn't that make it square?"

I thought he was out of health, irritable, disappointed that he had not made more of his own work, and jealous of my success, and I was willing to say anything to soften his feelings.

Howard simply turned away from me again, and I caught a mutter of "damned impertinence."

Seeing it was useless to say anything further at the moment, I strolled back into the centre of the room again, called Nous to me, and sat down.

"Jealous!" I thought, with contemptuous amusement; "how extraordinary!"

Then my thoughts rushed away in a sudden stream to Lucia, and I saw her face, glowing with delight, look out upon me from the blank surface of the wall.

"How soon now shall I possess you?" was my one thought. "How long to our marriage?"

I began by allowing three months, but I shortened and shortened the time till I cut it down to a fortnight.

"Could I persuade her to let it be in a fortnight?" and I

thought I could.

A quarter of an hour passed, and Howard had not moved from his position in the window. A very little day-dreaming is enough for me, especially about a woman. I yawned, stretched, and finally got up.

"Howard," I said, "I'm going out for a turn with Nous, but I will came back in time for dinner."

I lingered, but he said nothing. I put on my hat, called the dog, and went out. I started to walk to the Arc, and the distance there and back would have taken me, as I had said, till our dinner hour, but half way there the inclination failed. I felt tired and turned back.

"How utterly done up I feel!" I thought; "not worth anything. This last book has thoroughly taken it out of me. Rest! Rest! That was what I longed for now. My whole system seemed crying out for it. Of all the benefits the just-accomplished work would bring, celebrity, money, even, yes, even Lucia, seemed not so seductive in those moments as the possibility of gratifying this intolerable mental and physical craving for repose."

As I walked home a sense of tranquillity, a quiet, peaceful feeling of relief was transfused through me, and seemed communicated from the mind to the body and to every nerve of my frame, as if I were under the influence of some soothing drug.

I reached the hotel considerably before the time I had mentioned to Howard, and I supposed he would be out. However, as I came near I saw that our window was well lighted up. In fact, there seemed an unusually brilliant light in the room. Nous and I went up the stairs. He seemed to know and feel his master's good spirits, and kept licking my hand at intervals as he bounded up the stairs beside me, and then outstripping me, he would wait on the landing above me impatiently till I got there, in a hurry to race up the next flight.

As I opened my door a peculiar scent of smoke reached me, and the air was clouded and singularly warm. Howard was in the room, and I could not make out at first what he was doing. He was crouching on his heels in front of the grate and seemingly stirring or poking something beneath the bars. Some, I can hardly define what, instinct, guided my eyes to the side table where I had left my manuscript. It was gone. At that instant: the wind from the wide open window and door blew the lamp flame and stirred the curtains, and a great sheet of whole black tinder drifted across the carpet up to my feet.

Then I knew - he was burning, or had burnt, my work. A flame was dying down in the grate, filled and overflowing with ragged black fragments. With a curse I sprang towards the fender, but Nous was quicker than I. Either divining my intention, or made suspicious by the queer, sinister look Howard's figure had, the dog flew upon him with a growl, rolled him over and seized the clothing at his neck.

In another instant I would have called him off, but Howard was an inveterate coward. I saw his face turn livid with terror as the dog pinned his throat to the floor. His hand stretched out convulsively and grasped a long table knife that lay, together with the string that had held my manuscript, beside him on the floor. He seized it, and in an instant, before my eyes, he had plunged it deep into the breast of the dog standing over him. It was all done in a second - a flash. There was a gush of blood upon the floor, a broken moan from Nous, and then he staggered and fell over on his side - motionless.

Howard struggled breathless, white as death, to his feet. For one second I stood transfixed, watching him with blazing eyes. Then one step forward and I was upon him. My two hands closed like steel round his throat, and by his head, thus, I dragged him from the hearth out into the centre of the room.

"You unutterable, unspeakable cur and devil!" I muttered, and I saw his face blackening under my grip.

A gust of wind passed through the room, blowing to the door with a bang, and it whirled aloft, round us, broken and quivering pieces of black tinder. The air was full of them. And the dead dog lay in a pool of blood before us. It seemed to me that my brain was rocking with the fury and rage I felt - my whole frame convulsed in it. The loss, the irreparable loss, the killed hopes I saw in those floating ashes round me, came home to me till my brain seemed breaking asunder with anger. To murder him came the impulse! How? There were a thousand ways! To grind my fingers still deeper into his throat - THUS! THUS! Or that long knife that lay there on the rug, driven into and twisted round in his breast; or that sharp corner of the fender to batter out his brains; or drag him through the long, open window and hurl him in the darkness from that second floor balcony. Which? Devil! devil! Then as I held him there the thought pierced me, - Was I a brute to feel a blind rage like this? Had I ever in my life lost my own self-command, that command which sets us where we stand as men, as sane, highly-organised beings? And should a miserable, worthless cur like this have the power to break that self-control?

My whole pride and self-respect rose within me and commanded my passion back within its bounds. I unclosed my hands from his throat, and dropped him upon the ground as I would have dropped a loathsome rag. I watched him rise to his knees, trembling, livid, and terrified, and then scramble to his feet, with satisfaction that such a thing as he had not broken my own self-rule.

"Go out of this room," I said, and he hurried to the communicating door and shut and locked it securely after him.

I heard him do so with a contemptuous smile. Had I wanted to follow him, my weight flung against the flimsy door would have crushed it in. And I was left standing there alone in the smoke-filled room with nothing but the thunderings of my own pulses to break the silence.

"Inconceivable," I murmured, as the wind, stirring it, made the tinder creak in the grate as it lay in thick masses; "simply inconceivable."

I walked to the hearth and bent over the dog. He was already growing cold. He had not moved after his first fall. That vicious, brutal stab must have gone straight in to the heart. The knife was wet half way to the hilt. I lifted the dog and laid him on the sofa, and then mechanically went towards the blowing night-air and into the balcony. My brain seemed only just maintaining its right balance. So: all my labour, all my confident expectations, all the triumphant pleasure with which I had come back that afternoon, all the result of this past year's effort were now - nothing. Marked in a little floating dust. And not one vestige, not an outline nor portion of an outline even, remained. There was no rough draft, no sketch, no note or notes of the work existing. I always wrote every manuscript, from its first word to its last, on the paper that went to the publisher. My inspiration of the time was transferred direct to the page before me, and there it stood, without alteration, without correction. I never wanted to touch it or change it after it was once written. I was struck down, back again to the foot of the hill of work up which I had been struggling twelve months. Lucia, celebrity, pleasure, liberty, everything I coveted was now removed, taken far off into indefinite distance from me. For twelve months they had been coming nearer, steadily nearer, with each accomplished page, and to-day, only to-day, I had left the publisher's office knowing they were close to me, almost within my very arms. Like the prisoner serving his time in gaol, and living, as it were, in the last day that sets him free, I had been living these twelve months in the day when the last line should be written. Now all to be recommenced from the wearying, sickening beginning. And why? Why had he done it? That I could not understand. As a psychological enigma it leapt fitfully before my brain between the spasms of personal desperation. He had nothing to gain, everything to lose by my failure. He knew I was a man to always do the utmost for my friend, simply because he was my friend, and therefore from any increase of power in me he could derive nothing but benefit. There was absolutely no motive, could be no cause, for the act except undiluted jealousy and envy. I stepped inside the room again and went again to the hearth. Except when I saw the piles of black tinder I could not realise that he had done it. It seemed incredible, as if I must be dreaming. But there they lay, leaf upon leaf, some whole and perfect yet, sheets of black tinder, curled round at the corners where the flames had rolled them up, and lined still with white marks where the ink had been. Yes, it was so. The whole of my work was a nothing, and I a dependent pauper again.

Where was that whole brilliant structure now that I had lived for and so passionately loved through this past year? Along each line had flowed the very essence of my feelings at the time the line was written, and each one was irreplaceable. The fervour of a past inspiration, like the fervour of a past desire, can never be recalled. I gazed down into the grate and felt, stealthily creeping upon me, as if it had been a beast with me in the empty room, my intense hatred of this other man, divided from me by a few feet of space and one slight partition. There was no outlet from his room except into this. A few steps, force my way in, and what would follow?

I pressed both hands across my eyes and bowed my head till it leant hard upon the mantelpiece, feeling the longing and the urging towards physical violence against him rush upon me and tear me like wolves. The mental rage diffused itself through all the physical system till it seemed like poison pouring through my veins. Every pulse, beating convulsively in arms and chest and neck, seemed to clamour together in hungry fury. I leant there trying to stifle, to kill the thoughts that came and beat down the brutal rage. And as I stood there I heard Howard cough in the next room - that slight effeminate cough he gave when nervous or confused. I felt my blood leap at the sound, and it rushed in a scalding stream over my face. I raised my head and began mechanically to pace the room.

Even now it hardly seemed real, and my eyes kept returning and returning to the console where the manuscript had always lain out of work hours through the past year. "Devil! devil!" I muttered at intervals; "what an unutterable devil." I don't know how long I walked up and down, but suddenly a sense of physical fatigue, of collapse, forced itself upon me. I threw myself in the corner of the couch and took the dog's dead head upon my knee. Dead! It seemed strange - the constant companion of ten years. I had had him from his first earliest days.

Even before his eyes had opened I was struck by the intelligent way he had lain at his mother's side, and surnamed him Nous on the spot, after my favourite quality. I admit, like all good intelligences, because they have always their own particular views on everything, he had given a great deal of trouble. He had gnawed up my important business letters when cutting his teeth; he had made beds on my new light spring suits; he had sucked his favourite, most greasy mutton bone on the couch where my best manuscript lay drying; and out of doors he strongly objected to follow.

It is extremely annoying on a hot August afternoon, when you have just time to catch the Richmond train, and a friend is with you, to have your collie suddenly start off at a gallop in the opposite direction to the station, and pay absolutely no attention to the most distracted whistling and calling. Nothing for it but to start in pursuit, to run yourself into a fever, and after lapse of time to return with the fugitive to find your train missed and your friend as savage as a bear.

"If that dog were mine I'd thrash him within an inch of his life!" was the usual remark when I got back.

"Then I am extremely glad he is not yours," I used to answer, fastening on the dog's collar, and making him walk at the end of a foot of chain as a punishment.

"You'll never teach him like that, Vic. If you gave him a good kick in the eye now he'd remember it!"

"Thanks very much for your advice," I returned, "but I should never forgive myself if I kicked any animal in the eye."

"You are a queer, weak-hearted sort of fellow!" was the general answer, in a contemptuous tone, at which I used to shrug my shoulders and continue to manage my dog in my own way.

He would remember a blow, a kick, or a thrashing. I knew that. And that was exactly what I meant to avoid, whatever it cost at times to keep my temper with him. Besides, in all physical violence towards another object there is a peculiar, dangerous, seductive fascination. Once indulged in at all, it grows rapidly and imperceptibly into a positively delicious pleasure and habit, just as, if never indulged in, there grows up an always increasing horror and loathing of it.

Rage and anger, and their physical expression, become by habit a sort of joy, similar to the joy in intoxication, but if only the habit can be formed the other way there is an equal joy obtainable from self-restraint.

Control of the strongest passions is supposed to be difficult to attain, but the whole difficulty lies in laying the first stones of its foundation. If this is done the fabric will then go on building itself. Day by day a brick will be added to the walls, until finally no shock can overthrow them.

More and more as a man holds in his passions, more and more as he feels the pride of holding all the reins of his whole system firmly in his hand, will he have an abhorrence of scattering them to the idle winds at the bidding of the first fool who chances to vex him. But if he forms the habit of holding those reins so loosely that they drag along in the mud, and are trampled on at every instant, more and more difficult is it to gather them up.

The man who begins striking his dog as a punishment will proceed to kick it when it comes accidentally in his way, and then go on to knocking it about, simply because he feels in a bad humour.

So I never would, when I came back from these chasings, crimson, heated, breathless, made to look like a fool, and excessively annoyed altogether, cheat myself with the excuse that Nous wanted correction, or any other nonsense to cover my own ill-temper. As a matter of fact, he soon learnt it was uninteresting to be brought back to the very same corner from where he had started and have to walk all the rest of the way at the end of a scrap of chain, and his education passed happily over without a single rough word. It took longer perhaps than a treatment by blows, but I had my reward.

The dog conceived a limitless, boundless affection for me which more than repaid me. Some men, of course, don't want affection. They only care for obedience, and not at all how it is attained.

For myself I can see no pleasure in being merely dreaded. I should hate to see anything - man, woman, servant, dog, anything - start in terror at my footstep; hate to feel I brought gloom wherever I came, and left relief behind me.

Nous was extremely quick-witted, and it used to amuse me enormously the way he behaved when, as sometimes happened, I trod upon his foot accidentally, or fell over him in the dark. Knowing that he had never had a voluntary blow from me in his life, he would leap enthusiastically over me and lick my hands after his first yelp, as much as to say -

"Yes; I know it was quite an accident. I know, I am sure you didn't mean it."

We had been inseparable, he and I, for these ten years. He had walked by my side, eaten from my plate, slept on my bed, and his death now in my service left a heavy, jagged-edged wound.

As I sat there in the corner of the couch, with my hand absently stroking the glossy black coat, there came the very soft jarring of a key in the lock.

I glanced towards Howard's door. The sound continued. The key was being very slowly and gently turned, and then the handle was grasped and cautiously revolved. He evidently hoped I was asleep, and wanted to enter without disturbing me. I sat in silence with my eyes on the door, which slowly opened.

Howard stood on the threshold. He saw I was sitting there facing him, and he seemed to pause, unable to come forward or retreat. He did not look particularly happy as a result of his work. His face was pallid and haggard. Fool! to have flung away a valuable friend, and shackled himself with the fear of another man!

"What do you want?" I said, as he did not move.

"My manuscripts, Victor. I left them here."

"There they are on the table. They are quite safe. Did you think I should act as you have? Come and take them if you want them."

He had to pass close before me to do so, and I watched his nervous, hurried approach to the table, and the trembling of his hand as he gathered up the papers, with contemptuous eyes.

When he had grasped them all in his hand he gave an involuntary side look at me and the motionless form beside me - a look that he seemed unable to abstain from giving, though against his will. I met his glance, and he hurried away back to his own door, and went through it as a leper will shuffle and shamble away out of one's sight.

As soon as the morning came, I left the hotel without having tried the vain attempt of sleep, and did not return to it till the evening. At noon I called upon the publisher and explained that an unfortunate accident had occurred, and the MS. I had received back from him yesterday had been destroyed.

At that he beamed upon me blandly, and remarked that such a thing was unfortunate, but that without doubt M'sieur would make all haste to re-copy it, and would let him have a new draft as soon as possible.

I shook my head, feeling my lips and throat grow dry as I answered -

"That which you had was the original, not a copy. I have no copy of it from which I can replace it."

"But M'sieur will certainly have his notes, his private work, his first scheme?"

"None. I do not work in that way. There is not a scrap of paper relative to it anywhere."

Upon this the publisher rose, looked at me in a long silence, and then said in an icy tone, -

"Then M'sieur wishes me to understand that he does not intend to allow our firm to publish his work at all?"

I flushed at the insult his words contained. They practically intimated that he thought the whole thing an invention, and that I was going to give the MS. elsewhere. I got up too, and said -

"I have told you the MS. is destroyed, and I have no means of reproducing it, therefore it is impossible for it to be brought out by your or any other firm."

The man before me merely raised his shoulders over his ears, bowed, spread out the palms of his hands, raised his eyebrows, and muttered, -

"Comme vous voulez, M'sieur."

Confound him! was he a liar that he assumed me to be one.
There was nothing to do but to bow and leave.

As I walked out of his office into the fresh, sparkling, morning
sunlight, life to me had a very bitter savour. I walked through
the streets till I felt tired in every muscle. Then I sat thinking
on a bench in a green corner of the Champs Elysees, watching
absently the sun patches jump from leaf to neighbouring leaf as
the wind elevated and depressed them, and trying to mentally
seize upon and analyse this vile, low impulse of another man's
envy.

It was dark when I came back to the hotel. When I came up to
my room I was surprised to see quite a little crowd of figures
clustered round my door, all talking at once in their shrill
French tones, all gesticulating at each other as if about to tear
off each other's scalps.

Angry exclamations reached me as I came towards them.

"Mais je vous dis, je ne savais pas!"

"Mais c'est impossible!"

"Pas en regie!"

"Que voulez vous? C'est un barbare!"

Then as I came up there was a general cry of "Le voila! le
voila!" and in an instant they were all around me, all
clamouring, screaming, questioning me at once. The master of
the hotel in the greatest agitation, the manager in his shirt
sleeves, two or three waiters, a man looking like a gendarme,
and another official with a paper in his hand. For a second
they shouted so - nothing could be distinguished except

broken phrases and the continual repetition of the words "Notification" and "M'sieur le Commissionaire."

"A vous la responsibilite!"

"Moi? je n'en savais rien!"

"Il veut abimer notre sante!"

"Il partera tout de suite!"

I looked at them for a moment in amaze, and the fellow with the paper thundered out - "Silence," which produced the effect of cold thrown suddenly in boiling water. The little crowd pressed in upon me closely and listened awe-struck as the Commissionaire spoke to me, in French, of course.

"Monsieur," he said, in an impressive tone, "I am informed you have a dog here!"

I nodded.

"A dog - dead!" and the accent on the last word was terrific.

"My dog unfortunately has died," I said. "Yes" - and I wondered more and more the upshot of it all.

"Then," thundered the official, purple with excited rage, "how is it, Monsieur, you have not sent a notification to the police?"

I was fairly taken aback. The matter, though I barely yet comprehended it, was evidently, in their estimation, one of serious importance. Involuntarily, I glanced round at the others as the Commissionaire scowled threateningly at me. They noted my glance, and attributing it, I suppose, to guilty confusion, there were suppressed and complacent murmurs all round me, and shakes of the head.

"Pas d'explication!"

"Vous voyez ca?"

"Point d'excuse!"

"It is scandalous, it is shameful, it is abominable, M'sieur," shouted the Commissionaire, "the way you have acted! Twenty-four hours you hide the dead body of a dog in your bedroom! You hope to escape the eye of the law! You would bring disgrace on the gendarmerie, on the municipality of Paris! You laugh at our regulations, M'sieur, you laugh!" and he brandished the paper violently. "But you will find the authority of France is greater than you! There are cells, M'sieur, there are courts, there are judges for your education!!!"

Matters were apparently growing serious for me. I had evidently offended them all desperately somehow. "You go out in the morning," he continued, furiously, "and you do not slink back here till it is dark! You are a coward, M'sieur! a coward!"

No Englishman likes hearing himself abused, and my own anger now was considerably roused. But still, in my way about life, I have found the inestimable value of conciliation. It saves one such an infinity of trouble. I suppose I lean naturally towards it. At any rate, I always feel this - that if you have not the power on your side it is undignified to assume that which you cannot enforce, and if you have the power you can then afford to be civil.

A pleasant manner has never once failed me in bringing about an effect which is highly convenient to oneself, and in the long run it spares one's vanity considerably. There is hardly any human being, however aggressive he may be at first, that does not melt into respect before an imperturbable civility. I felt in this case, too, that I was probably in the wrong from their point of view. It was the question of another country's ways, and I have a lenient feeling towards the epichortyon. So, annoyed and irritated as I was, I checked my own feelings and said, -

"I think it is altogether a misunderstanding! I have no intention of breaking any regulations. I was not aware that a dog's death would be a matter where the law would interfere."

The fury on the purple face opposite me subsided somewhat.

"Is it then possible," he said, more quietly, "that you are in ignorance of our rule, that, when any animal dies in a private dwelling-house, the fact shall be notified within twelve hours to the police, in order that the dead body may be immediately removed?"

All eyes fixed upon me with breathless uncertainty.

"Certainly," I said, "I did not know of the regulation. If I had, I should have complied with it. There is no similar rule in England."

A great change took place in the official's manner. His face cleared, and he waved his arm with a gesture of magnificent condescension. His whole attitude expressed clearly that so enlightened and cultured a person as himself was in the habit of making every allowance for any poor, benighted pagan like me.

"Well, M'sieur; well, I accept your statement, and I withdraw my expressions of a moment back. But think, M'sieur, of the risk to which your conduct has exposed others. Think of the pollution of the air, the contamination of the atmosphere! Think, M'sieur, of the typhoid! the fever!! the cholera!!!"

He looked round upon the others, and a sympathetic shudder of horror passed over them.

As an Englishman, of course, I felt strongly inclined to derisive laughter. However, I merely said, -

"Well, what is to be done next?"

"The body must be removed, M'sieur!" he answered, with a touch of severity, "at once!!"

"How?"

"A scavenger will remove it."

I stood silent. The idea repelled me. This thing that had been petted and cared for by me for ten years, had slept at my side, and often been held in my arms, now to be flung upon a dust heap, with the rotting matter of a Paris street. The mind will not change its associations so quickly. I looked at the man and said, -

"Can I not bury the dog somewhere myself?"

"I am afraid - I hardly know - " he said. "These are the rules, - that all dead animals are taken by the municipality."

He spoke reluctantly now. His personal animosity against me was evidently dead. Fortunate that I had not offended him earlier in the interview; if I had, he would certainly now have dragged the dog from me with every species of indignity and insult, and I could have done nothing against him, armoured up as he was with the law. As things stood, he was clearly on my side.

"Perhaps this gentleman," I said, indicating the master of the hotel, "would let me purchase a piece of ground for a grave in his courtyard. If so, would you allow me to bury the dog there?"

The master of the hotel, who saw now that after all there would be no serious row with the police, nor discredit on his hotel, and began to think his fury had been somewhat misdirected, hastened to assure me that I need not consider the matter; that not only was a portion, but the whole courtyard at my disposition, and not as a purchase, but as a free gift, if M'sieur le Commissionaire sanctioned the proceeding.

The official hesitated, and the onlookers, their sympathies engaged, murmured, -

"Ah, pauvre chien!"

"C'est l'affection vois-tu?"

"Il aime le chien, c'est naturel!"

"L'affection, c'est toujours touchante!"

The Commissionaire, his own inclination thus backed up by the prevailing sentiment, turned to me, and said -

"Well, M'sieur, I ought to take your dog from you, but still, as you say you will bury the dog yourself, and, as I am sure this gentleman will see that the grave is deep enough to protect the health of the public, I believe I may safely grant you the permission you ask. It is accorded, M'sieur!" and he bowed, full of satisfied amiable authority and friendly feeling.

I held out my hand to him on the impulse.

"I am extremely obliged to you!"

He grasped it warmly in his, and laid his left effusively on his heart.

"You have my sincere sympathy, M'sieur."

Then lifting his hat and bowing, and putting out of sight the formidable document he had shaken in my face, he retreated down the corridor, followed by the other official, and leaving the hotel manager with me.

"I will have a grave dug at once, M'sieur," he said; "and you shall be informed when it is ready."

I thanked him and entered my own room.

A good three hours later I was following the gardener downstairs, the dead body of Nous, wrapped completely in one of my overcoats, in my arms. We went into the courtyard. It was raining now, the night quite dark, and a gusty wind blowing. We crossed the yard to where a broad flower-bed was planted. Here a grave, wide and deep enough for a human being, had been dug. A lantern, in which the flame blew fitfully, was set on the huge heap of mould and sent an uncertain light over the grave. I got down into it, and laid Nous gently, still wrapped in the coat, on the damp earth, with a heavy heart.

I vaulted out of the grave and stood, while the man filled it in, listening to the steady fall of the earth and its dull thud, thud. The rain came down steadily, and the man looked at me and said -

"Monsieur will be drenched through, he had better go within."

"No, no," I said; "continue."

And I waited while he dug away the mound, and the chilly wind rattled the branches of a tree near, and the rain soaked with a monotonous splashing into the earth, and the light flickered, barely strong enough to show me the man's working figure. When he had finished, when the grave was filled and the upper soil smoothed over, I turned and, mentally and physically chilled, went slowly back into the hotel. As I entered the gas-lit corridor I saw a figure there at the door. It was Howard. He was still in the hotel, and though I detested his proximity even, I had no influence on his departure. He was evidently hanging about there waiting for somebody or something, and to my intense indignation, as he caught sight of me, he came towards me.

"Oh, Victor," he said hurriedly, in an uncertain tone, "I must speak to you!"

What intolerable insolence to dare to come to me, the man he had so mortally injured. My impulse was to stretch out my right arm and fell him to the ground with a blow that should have the force of my whole system in it. The colour came hot in all my face.

"Pray don't let us have a scene here," I said, coldly.

"Very good, then come outside. It is only for a few seconds. You always used to say you would never refuse to hear a person once, whatever they had done."

It was my principle, as he said, and I controlled the loathing I had of him, of his voice, his look, his presence, and said -

"Come out, then," and we went down to the door.

There was an alley just outside the hotel, a cul de sac, black and empty. Down this we turned, and when we had passed the side door of the hotel he spoke.

"Victor, I am awfully sorry about the MS.; I am really. I would give worlds to replace it now if I could. I have been utterly wretched since. Is there anything I can do now to help you?"

"No," I said bitterly, "you cannot re-write my manuscript nor resuscitate my dog."

"Oh, why did I do it? I can't think! I can't understand it! If you knew what I have felt since!"

"Have you nothing more to say than this?" I asked; "because this sort of thing is useless and leads to nothing."

"But what do you think of me? You hate me! But it was not premeditated, I swear. I had no motive, no gain in doing it, and we have been great friends always; but I suppose that can never be again now! But still it was an impulse, a sudden impulse, only because I was so jealous of you! It was irresistible at the moment! The thing was in flames before I realised it!

You know yourself what impulse is! You always knew I was like that!"

"Impulse!" I repeated. "Yes, I knew you were impulsive, but that such an impulse could ever come to you as that - to burn, irreparably destroy the year's work, and all the hopes of a man who was an intimate friend, and against whom you had never had the shadow of a complaint, that I never could have believed! Impulse! It is not one that I can conceive existing except in hell!"

We were talking with voices moderated, rather low than otherwise; but the hatred I felt of him I let come into each word and edge it like a knife.

He drew in his breath.

"Then our friendship is at an end?" he said, in a weak nervous tone.

"Utterly. As if it had never been. You have cut out its very roots. I had a great friendship for you - more, a great affection. It would have stood a great deal. I would have passed over many injuries that you might have done. Anything almost but this, that you knew was so completely blasting to all my own desires. This shows me what your feelings must have been at the time, at any rate, and remember a thick manuscript is not burnt in a minute. How long must it have taken you to destroy those sheets upon sheets of paper in which you knew another man's very heart, and blood, and nerve had been infused? All that time you must have been animated with the sheer lust of cruelly and brutally ill-using and injuring me, and in return I" -

I shut and locked my lips upon the words that rose.

To abuse or curse another is almost as degrading to oneself as to strike him.

We had come up to the end of the alley now, and we paused by the blank brick wall. There was a lamp projecting from it which threw some light upon us both, and, as his figure came distinctly before my eyes, I felt one intolerable desire to leap upon him - this miserable creature who had destroyed my work - fling him to the ground, and grind his face and head to a shapeless mass in this slimy gutter that flowed at our feet.

Could he have faintly realised what my feelings were, coward as he was, he would never have come up this empty alley with me.

"Well, Victor, I am leaving Paris to-night; but I felt I could not go without telling you how infinitely I regret it all. If you can never be my friend again, you can forgive me. Let me hear you say that you do before I go."

Forgive him! Great God! Forgive an injury so wanton, so excuseless! Every savage instinct in me leapt up at the word.

The manuscript! I felt inclined to shout to him. The manuscript! Give that back to me and then come and talk about forgiveness. Had the act and the motive been as loathsome, but the injury, the actual injury, the positive loss to me been less, I could have forgiven; but the blow was so sharp, the damage so irremediable, I could not. Even at his words I seemed to see staring me in the face the months of toil awaiting me before I could rebuild - if I could ever - the fabric he had destroyed in half-an-hour.

And crowding upon this came the thought of what he had robbed me of, the name, the freedom, the power that those vanished paper pages had been pregnant with for me. He was leaving Paris, he said; and so might I have been leaving free and successful, leaving to return to Lucia, but for him.

And now I was to remain - remain here, a prisoner, to work on another twelve weary months at that most nauseating of tasks, repairing undone work. To recommence, to take up the old burden, to start it all over again, now when I had just made myself free! To be shackled again with the weight of uncertainty and expectancy for another year, through him, and by God he talked of forgiveness! - to me! - now!

It was too soon. Later - later, perhaps, when I was calmer, when some of the injury had been repaired, when a spark of hope had been rekindled; then, if he asked, but now - The days before me stretched such a bitter, hopeless blank! And how did I know that his act could ever be nullified! It might so turn out that now I never should accomplish my end.

My health had worn thin and my brain was tired out. Either might give way, and then - a life blasted through him! Brute and devil! that was what he had wished, and was perhaps wishing still, even now, when he professed to be so anxious for forgiveness. I glanced towards his face opposite me, but it was too dark to see its expression. A slight, steady drizzle fell between us; I only saw his slight figure before me in the uncertain light, and again something urged me.

Take your revenge now while you can get it. This man may have spoiled all your life, but when you realise it, then he may be away and out of your power. Thrash him! Half kill him now while you have the chance! But I did not stir. Vengeance has always seemed to me a poor thing. Supposing . . . After? . . . If I satiated my rage then, what after. I should have two things to regret instead of one. No. Let him go with his vile act upon his head.

But forgive? I could not. He had taken the inside, the best of my life, and I hated, purely hated him. I turned a step aside, his mere outline before my eyes sent the hate running hotly through me.

"I can't," I muttered; "no, I can't."

Howard sprang forward and put his hand on my arm, and at the touch I seemed to abhor him more.

"Victor, I wish I could say how I regret it. I wish I could express myself, but I can't. If you knew - I would cut off my right hand now to undo it! I would indeed!"

"Who wants you right hand" I said, savagely, stopping and turning on him as I shook off his detestable touch. "Fool! You can talk now! Replace a single chapter of that book I slaved at - that would be more to the purpose!"

Howard's face grew paler. I saw that, even in the darkness.

"It is not open to me, Victor, now," he said; "but it is still open to you to forgive."

His voice had a grave significance in it. No words that he could have chosen would have been better. The short, quiet sentence was like a sword to divide my hatred, and penetrate to the better part of man. The truth, the unerring force, the reflections of this life's chances and decrees in those words went home. It was not open to him now to repair; later, it might not be open to me to forgive. And later, when all these present vivid feelings were swept away in the past, should I not wish I had forgiven.

I stood silent, and the query went through me - What is forgiveness? Is it to feel again as we have felt before the injury? This is impossible. Do what I would that affection I had had for him could never re-awaken. It was stamped out, obliterated, as a flower is ground into the dust beneath one's heel.

Still the loathing and the hatred I had for him now would pass. Years would cancel it all, and bring with them mere indifference towards him, the thought of him and of his act. To say the words now, and let the time to come slowly fill them with truth, was better, surely, than to reiterate my hatred of him - hatred which years hence would seem almost foolish to me myself.

"I can't think that my forgiveness can be of very serious import to you," I said quietly. "However, it is yours."

"You will shake hands with me, then, won't you?" and he held out his hand.

With an effort I stretched out mine and took his, and held it for a second as in old times.

"Good-bye, Victor," he said, in rather a strained voice, "I shall never cease to regret what I have done."

He hesitated, as if wondering if I should speak. I did not, and he turned and went down the alley, and the darkness closed up after him. I leant silent against the wall, hating myself for forgiving him and letting him go, and yet knowing I would do the same again.

"One must forgive, one must forgive; otherwise one is no better than brute," I thought mechanically. "Later I shall be glad," - and similar phrases by which Principle excuses itself to furious, disappointed Nature.

After a time I grew calmer, and I went back to the hotel and up to my room. It seemed emptier, blanker still, now that even the dead body of the dog had gone. In the grate, and scattered over the carpet, remained still remnants of black tinder. I felt suddenly tired, worn out. I flung myself, dressed as I was, upon the bed, and lay there in a sort of stupor. And the slow, dark hours of that terrible night of depression tramped over me with leaden footsteps.

CHAPTER V

The next morning, just as I had dropped into an uneasy doze, there came a knocking and a hammering, and a muttering outside my door.

"M'sieur! M'sieur!" Tap-tap-tap. "Que diable donc! Qu'il dort! M'sieur! Profondement! Est ce qu'il est mort? Ah! c'est une bete Anglaise!" Tap-tap-tap.

All this came through the wall in a hazy sort of confusion, mingling with my sleep, before it roused me to go and open the door. Finally, however, I stumbled off the bed and unlocked the door, and threw it open.

"What now" I thought. "Have I broken any more of your confounded Gallic regulations."

It was not a Commissary of Police this time, but a uniformed commissionaire, with a note in his hand. Possibly serenely unconscious that I had heard his polite remarks outside, he bowed urbanely.

"Bonjour, M'sieur! A thousand apologies for disturbing M'sieur! But Madame said I was to deliver this note personally."

I looked at him with elevated eyebrows. I knew no Madame in Paris.

"I think there is some mistake," I said.

"But why? Monsieur Eeltone? Numero quinze, is it not?"

"Hilton. Yes, that is my name."

He gave me a triumphant glance, and handed me the note with a flourish. The envelope was that of the Grand Hotel; but the writing on it was Lucia's writing. Lucia here in Paris! Close to me! How? Why? The blood poured over my face. With a sense of delight I tore the envelope open: -

"I am at the above hotel. I shall remain at home all to-day in the hope that you may be able to come and see me."

"LUCIA."

I looked up the man in the doorway bowed with a deprecating air.

"Madame said I was to wait for an answer."

He had a subdued smile upon his face, which seemed to say - "We know all about these little notes! We are accustomed to them here in Paris!"

I told him to enter, and he followed me into the room and took an interested glance round. Probably, to his view, my pallid face and blood-shot eyes, my last night's clothes, my boots on my feet, and the bed unslept-in, conveyed the idea of a drunken fit only just over in time to make room for the morning's intrigue. A young, beautiful English madame - for the title Miss is barely recognised, never understood in Paris - staying at the hotel and sending notes to a young English M'sieur in another. Yes, this was plainly an intrigue of the genuine order, and the mari would doubtless arrive from England later. All was plain, and he stood with a patronising smile by the table, while I scribbled a note to Lucia.

"My Dearest Life, - I am rushing, flying to you now. I will be with you as soon as fiacre can bring me."

"VICTOR."

I closed it, and made him wait while I sealed it, lest he should interfere with it. Then I handed it to him with a two-franc piece, and with bon jours and remerciments and grins he withdrew.

I dressed hurriedly and yet carefully, and shaved with a dangerously trembling hand. The first fiacre that was passing as I left the hotel I took, and was driven, through the bright sunshine that filled the Paris boulevards, to the Grand. I sat back in it, with my arms folded, feeling my heart like a stone within me. Lucia's coming, that, thirty-six hours back, would have infused the extreme of delight through me, was now useless, worthless.

I could do nothing, say nothing. I was a prisoner again, fettered, bound, as if I had an iron collar on my neck, and manacles on my wrists. I looked through the shining, quivering sunlight that fell on every side with blank, unseeing eyes, and the bitterest curses against Howard rose to my lips, checked only by the knowledge that I had forgiven him.

When I reached the hotel, and mentioned her name, I was shown up to a private sitting-room on the first floor, facing the gay Paris boulevard, and with the bright light streaming in through its half-closed persiennes. A figure rose at the opening of the door, and came towards me with outstretched hands.

"Lucia!"

My eyes fixed on her, and my glance rushed over her in a second, and poured with feverish haste their report back into my brain. Within the first moment of my entry of the room, I was conscious of, I recognised that there was a great change, an almost indefinable, but nevertheless distinctly perceptible, metamorphosis in this woman since I had seen her last. Lucia was a somnambulist no longer. She had awakened. It was a lovely, living woman who crossed the room to me now; a woman awake to her own powers, conscious of the sceptre, and the gifts, and the kingdom that Nature puts into the hands of a woman for a few years, I felt all this as I looked at her, saw it in her advance towards me, heard it in the soft tones of her voice as she said, -

"Well, Victor, are you glad I have come?"

And it was with my heart suddenly beating hard, and my face pale, and a mist before my eyes, that I came forward to her. What had been the first slight shock to her sleeping woman's passions I had no idea.

Perhaps some chance glance from a man's eyes upon her as she passed him in a crowd had suddenly struck through the ice of her abstraction. Perhaps some pressure of an arm meaning she did not even comprehend. Perhaps some word, overheard between two men, whose meaning she did not even comprehend. Perhaps it was only Nature unaided that had whispered to her, - "Life is passing, and its greatest pleasure is as yet untried. Get up and seek it."

Perhaps any of these, or all or none. I could not say. The change was there. Lucia was conscious, awake. Pure, delicate, as from her integral nature she would always, but still awake. As she stood, the sun fell upon her light hair and seemed to get tangled there, a hot, rose glow was in her face, and the smooth scarlet lips parted in a faint seducing smile.

"Now, tell me everything," she said, softly, "I am sure the manuscript is finished by now."

She pointed to a wicker chair for me, and drew one just opposite it in which she threw herself, full in the morning light, but just avoiding the stabbing sun-rays. I saw in a sort of mechanical manner the way in which she was dressed. It was as a woman only dresses once or twice, perhaps, in her lifetime; and that is when she is determined to win, through the sheer strength and force of her beauty, in the face of every obstacle, the man she desires.

Every detail had been thought of, every beauty of her form studied and enhanced, from the light curls on her forehead, and the curves of her bosom rising and falling under its lace bodice, to the tiny shoes that came from beneath the folds of her delicate-coloured skirt.

It was presumably of cotton, for Lucia herself had informed me that she never wore anything in the mornings except cotton or serge; if so, it was a glorified cotton of a clear rose tint. Film upon film of lace hung over it in transparent folds, through which the glowing colour deepened and blushed at her slightest movement, as the hot colour in the heart of a rose flushes through all its leaves.

Above her supple hips, clasping her waist, shone an open-work band of Maltese silver, and above this rose delicate vase-like lines, swelling and expanding at last into the rounded curves of her bosom; here the colour seemed to glow deeper and warmer where her heart was beating tumultuously, and then towards her neck it paled again, beneath ruffle and ruffle of lace that lay like foam against the soft, snow-white throat. It was a symphony of colour. A perfect harmony of perfect tones in union with the brilliant fairness of her skin. The sleeves, half open to the elbow, revealed a white, rounded, downy arm, and the thousand subtle pink-and-white tints of her flesh seemed to melt and merge themselves into a bewildering, distracting glow within that rose-hued sleeve. She made one exquisite, intoxicating vision to the senses. In those moments I can hardly say I saw her. She rather seemed to sway before the dizzy sight of my excited eyes.

Dimly yet keenly, vaguely yet convincingly, I felt she had come as an adorable antagonist to my resolutions. Traditionally speaking, such a knowledge should have made me instantly on my guard.

I ought certainly to have summoned my control, my judgment, and so on, to say nothing of an icy reserve. But I did not. My whole heart seemed to rush out to her, my whole being to strain towards her. I longed to take her entirely in my arms, to kiss her on the lips and throat, and say, -

"Ask whatever you will and it shall be granted."

"The manuscript is finished, isn't it?" she repeated.

Oh, bitter, bitter, and cruel fate that had dragged the fruits of my labour, and with them everything, out of my hand!

"It was finished, Lucia, a few days ago," I said, speaking calmly with a great effort; "but an accident happened and it was destroyed."

I felt myself growing paler and paler as I spoke, meeting her lovely, eager eyes fixed on mine.

"Destroyed?" she echoed, growing white to the lips. "Oh, Victor! How?"

"I would rather not say, Lucia, exactly how it occurred, but it had been accepted by a publisher here, and I was going to make one or two trifling alterations in it to please him, and so I had it back. Well, then, as I say, something happened, and the thing was destroyed."

There was a dead silence.

I saw her heart beating painfully beneath the laces on her bosom, and pain stamped on all her face. Then she said abruptly, -

"Have you Howard with you still?"

"No. He left Paris last night," I answered.

Her eyes met mine full across the sunlight. We looked at each other in silence.

She asked nothing farther.

I believe she comprehended the whole case as it stood, because she would know that had I lost or injured the MSS. myself I should have no reason for concealing it. As a matter of honourable feeling I wanted to keep the fact from her, but I could not help her guessing it. Curiously enough her next question, after a long pause - though I did not see that in her mind there could have been connection between the subjects - was:

"Where is Nous?"

"Nous is dead."

"How did he die?"

"That, also, I would rather not say."

At that, in addition to a sharper look of distress, a puzzled surprise came into her face. She raised her delicate eyebrows and looked at me with a perplexed, half-frightened expression.

"Victor," she said, leaning forward a little in her chair, "was it he that tore up the manuscript? and did you kill him in a fit of rage?"

I looked back at her, also with surprise, that she could suggest such a thing of me as possible.

"Oh, no!" I said hastily; "nothing at all of the sort. No! If either the loss of the book or the dog's death had occurred in any way through my fault I would tell you. I have no secrets of my own from you, but both of these concern another man, and therefore I would rather let them pass."

There was silence.

Then I asked, looking at her, -

"Are you alone here, Lucia?"

"Except, of course, for my maid - Yes."

My heart beat harder. Why? I hardly know, except that the word "alone" has such a charm in it connected with a woman we love.

"Of course," she said, leaning back, "it is a little unconventional my coming here alone; but Mama was not well enough, and I - Victor," she said, with a sudden indrawn breath, "I felt I must come and see you. I told her I felt I should die there if they would not let me come!"

I saw her breast heave as she spoke, her cheek flushed and paled alternately, the azure of her eyes deepened slowly as the pupils widened in them, till there seemed midnight behind the lashes.

I felt a dangerous current stirring in all my blood at her words, a dry spasm seemed in my throat, blocking all speech.

"I thought you must have finished by now, and I came to say - I came to say" - she murmured.

The blood rushed scarlet, staining all the fair skin, across the face before me, and the bright lips fluttered in uncertain hesitation.

I guessed the situation.

She had come to say to me phrases that seemed quite easy, quite simple to her, murmuring them to herself in the silence of an empty studio, and now face to face with me, listening and expectant, they had become difficult, impossible. I leant forward, the blood hot in my own cheek, a dull flame waking in every vein.

"Darling," I said, taking her soft left hand within both my own, "I cannot tell exactly what you wish to tell me; but listen - I had finished all, and had things not turned out as they have I should have been starting now to come to you and say, 'Lucia I am free now to be your slave.' All this year we have been separated I have thought only of you, waking and sleeping, longed for you, dreamed of you, lived in the hour of our re-union, desired with an intensity beyond all words that day that gives you to me; and, forty hours back, that day, Lucia, seemed so near, but now - dearest" -

I stopped, choked, suffocated with the weight of hopeless, despairing passion that fell back upon itself within me.

Lucia leant forward, the beating, palpitating bosom was close to me, her white, nerveless hand lay close in mine.

"And now, Victor?"

"Now all is vanished. I am exactly in the position where I was when I left you in England a year ago."

"And what do you mean - what are we - what?" -

"My sweet, what can we do? I must recommence. I must work on another year."

I felt the burning, tremulous fingers grow cold in mine. Her face paled till it was like white stone. Then suddenly she withdrew her hand from my clasp, and started to her feet.

"Victor, I cannot! no, I cannot! I cannot wait another year! It will kill me!" she said, passionately, looking away from me, and pacing a short length of the floor backwards and forwards before me, as I rose, too, and stood watching dizzily the incomparable figure pass and repass, hardly master of myself.

"Dearest," she continued; "this is what I came to say - let us marry now. I thought you would have successfully finished your work, and we might do so; but now, now, even as it is, let it be as it is, let it be unfinished, and still, still let us marry. There is no real bar as there might be. There is no question of wrong to any one. We are to be married - it cannot matter to any one when we are. Continue to work afterwards. I am willing to be second always, in every thing, to your work. But don't drive me from you altogether. Let me stay with you now I have come. Let us marry now - here. Let us go before some official - the Maire, or some one, or English consul, no matter whom - this afternoon! Victor, if not now, that day you desire will never come. I shall never be your own. Think how it has receded and receded into time! We have been engaged now more than three years!"

She paused in front of me, and lifted her face - brilliant, glowing, appealing - with an intensity of passionate, eager longing in it that defied her words to express. Her whole form quivered with excitement, till I saw the laces of her dress tremble. On the bodice beneath my eyes, the lace fell from the shoulders, and its folds on each side divided slightly in the centre, leaving a depression there in which the rose-colour glowed crimson. It riveted my eyes this line - this channel of colour burnt fiercely beneath my lids.

I could see nothing but it; it seemed everywhere, to fill the room, to scorch into my brain, this palpitating, throbbing, crimson line. That terrible impulse of blind excitement was rapidly drawing me into itself - the impulse that counts nothing, knows nothing, reckons nothing but itself; that will buy the present hour at any sacrifice - that accepts everything, ignores everything but that one moment it feels approaching. This impulse urged me, pressed me, strained violently upon me.

It left me barely conscious of anything except the absorbing longing to take her, draw her close, hard into my arms, and say, "Yes, let all go; from this day henceforward you are mine." But almost unconsciously to myself my reason rebelled against being thus thrust down and trampled upon by this sudden, brute instinct rushing furiously through my frame, and my reason clutched me and clung to me and maintained its hold, and, feeling myself wrenched asunder by these two opposite forces, I stood immovable and silent.

"Victor," she said, after a minute, and the warm, white uncertain hand sought mine again and held it, "I have been working hard since you left, and the canvas is nearly finished, but I am willing to relinquish it for the present, to let it go. In all this time you have been away from me I have been slowly learning that one's own life and one's own life's happiness is of more worth than these abstract ideas, than one's work or talent or anything else. I have been feeling that you and I are letting day after day go by and are working for a to-morrow that for us may never come. Is this your philosophy?"

I looked down on her as she clasped my hand and drew it up to her breast, her eyes were on mine, and all my mental perceptions were blinded and forced down under the pressure of the physical senses.

"Take me into your life, Victor. I swear I won't interfere with your work. Let me sit somewhere beside you all day long while you write, and let me lie all night long watching you while you write, if you like! Oh, do let me! do speak to me?"

She pressed my hand in, convulsively, upon her breast, until it seemed to be in the midst of tremulous warmth, close upon the throbbing heart itself. I could not think. Thought seemed slipping from me. I felt sinking deeper each minute into the quicksand of desire. Nothing seemed clear any longer. All within my brain was merged into one hot, clinging haze, in which still loomed the idea that I must not yield. It would be dishonourable to my father, disappointing to myself, destructive to my work. I could not realise it then, could not see it, but I knew and remembered in a dim way that it was so, that it had been so decided, and I must adhere to it.

"It is impossible, Lucia."

"Why?"

"Because I promised my father we should not marry until I had got out some book."

"But rescind the promise! Say that you cannot carry it out! Give up all help from him, and let us live our lives apart!"

"I have no means to do it with."

"You can make them! Surely with all your knowledge you can get some ordinary work to do till you can get your works out!"

"Even if I had the means I could not, after the understanding between us, after all he has done for me, throw him over at a moment's notice."

"He has no right to ask such a sacrifice!"

"It has all been thought out," I said dully, "and settled before. I can't re-argue it all now. I decided it finally before I left England, and I am in the same position now as I was then."

A scarlet colour stole into the rose glow on Lucia's face.

"You don't care for me, Victor!" she said passionately. "You can't! No man could and speak so!" and she threw my hand from her and herself into the long chair in a sudden, wild storm of excited tears.

I hardly knew what I was doing. I felt as if I had been struck sharply on the eyes as I heard her words. I fell on my knees beside her chair, and put both my arms up and clasped them round the soft waist, and let them lean hard on the hips, in a spasm of angry passion.

"What are you thinking of? You know there is nothing I covet like yourself," I said savagely, the blood flowing over my face as hotly as it burnt in her own. "But we can't do this. We should both despise ourselves afterwards. You should be the last person to urge it on me. What do I ask you? To wait another nine months! That's all. You should help me."

"Help you?" she said, her eyes blazing upon me with anger, shame and passion. "Help you in making a fatal mistake? No, I will not! You can refuse me if you like, but all the responsibility is with you. I warn you against it. I have come to warn you. When it is too late you will wish this day back again. You are not tied now after a whole year's work, and after a misfortune you could not help. If you always wait in life until you have settled and arranged everything just to your satisfaction you will find that you lose your desires. They will slip like sand through your hands while you are arranging your circumstances. Life is never, never quite as we would have it. We must take our pleasures one by one as they are offered to us; it is hopeless to think we can gain them all together. Oh, Victor dearest!" she added, stretching out two rounded, glowing arms in a sort of half-timid desperation and clasping them round my neck, while mine still held her heaving waist, "love now, and win your name by-and-by"

There was delirium in my brain. The whole woman's form swam before my sight. My arms locked themselves violently round the yielding, pulsating waist.

"I would if I could," I muttered, and that was as much as I could say.

"You can," she urged in a soft, desperate voice. "Why not? I can't believe you love me if you let me go back now."

"I can't believe you love me if you urge me to do what I think is dishonourable."

Her arms dropped from my neck.

"Oh, it is a mistake," she said.

"Perhaps so."

We had both risen. The floor seemed to bend beneath my feet. I felt her pulses still beating against my arms. I looked at her. Our eyes met, and the gaze seemed locked, fixed, and we neither of us could transfer it. My throat seemed rigid, dry as a desert; her voice was choked, suffocated in tears. But "Kiss me, at least; oh, kiss me!" was written on the whole imploring face, on the wildly quivering lips, in the burning, distracted eyes. But what use? Rather such a kiss, here, now, might bring an irremediable loss. In any case, the pain of parting after would be ten times intensified for us both. Could I then go? Would any force then be left in me? Would my will stand beyond a certain point? I did not know. It seemed the only safety for us both, the one rock still left in the wild ocean of our passion - an absolute denial to the rushing feelings to find expression in the least of acts or words.

I did not believe nor think she could misunderstand me. I felt sure the struggle and the suffering and the desire must be printed in my face. I knew she must see in it that I was not cold before the despairing, passionate longing I saw stirring all her pained, excited frame. To me it seemed as if she must see me ageing and my face lining before her eyes. I held her hand in mine hard for a moment. Then I dropped it gently, and she looked at me - stunned. And so, unkissed, untouched by my lips that ached so desperately for hers, I left her and went out through the passages and down the steps and out of the hotel into the brilliant streets with my nerves strung tense to sheer agony.

I had acted, of course, in a correct and orthodox manner. No one could reproach me for the interview just past, but in my heart there was a self-condemning voice. Pleasure seldom unveils her face and offers herself to us twice, and Venus is a dangerous goddess to offend. I said, "Wait, wait," and "tomorrow," but those ominous lines beat dully through my brain -

"to daurion tis oiden;
os oun et eudi estin."

When I reached my hotel, thought, intelligent thought, seemed collapsing, and my brain spinning round and round within my skull.

"The end of me," I muttered, "at this rate will certainly be a cell in a lunatic asylum."

For the first time, I released my rule against drugs. I sent the hotel porter for a draught of chloral. When it came I drank it, and, in the middle of the brilliant afternoon sunshine, threw myself on the bed, conscious of nothing but a longing for oblivion. Unaccustomed to it, the drug seized well upon me. For long, merciful, quiet hours I knew nothing.

After this there came a blank of many days: idle, barren days, in which I did nothing, knew nothing except that I suffered. My brain seemed blank, empty, like a quarry of black slate. The power that seemed to dwell there at times was gone now; crushed all that impersonal emotion of the writer's mind by the blighting personal emotion of the man.

A fortnight passed, and at the end of it I had done nothing; another week, and then another, and I had still not written a line.

At last one night, sitting idle in the cafe after dinner, I felt the old impulse stir in me, a rush of eager inclination to write went through me. A sudden sense of power filled me. The brain, empty and idle a few minutes before, became charged with energy and desire to expend it. A corresponding current of activity poured along each vein. The old familiar impetus swayed me.

I welcomed it gladly and went upstairs, got out paper and a pen, and the remembrance of my own life slipped away from me. All that night I wrote, and the next day, and the fresh manuscript was fairly started. For a whole fortnight I wrote almost incessantly. I snatched a little food in the cafe, hardly knowing what I ate.

The nights passed feverishly without sleep, while the brain revolved, excitedly, scenes written or to be written. Towards the end of the fortnight the impulses to work steadily declined. I forced myself to write at intervals; but, as usual, the forced work was worthless, and I destroyed it when it was done. No, it was no use. I could merely shrug my shoulders and smoke and wait.

The hot, blank days of August drifted by, and as I saw the boulevards empty themselves day by day, and Paris grow hotter and duller each afternoon, I felt the solitary existence weigh heavier and heavier upon me. The loss of the dog seemed to have made a larger gap in my existence than I should have believed; his unused collars still lay upon my mantelpiece, his plate and saucer still stood in the corner by the hearth, and sometimes when I was climbing the dark stairs at night to my empty room I felt as if I would have given years of my life to have had the dog leap up into my arms in welcome.

One of these nights, when I came into the unlighted room, I saw a letter lying, a white square, in the dusk, upon the table. I supposed it was from my father, as Lucia never wrote, and I was too occupied, or indifferent, or rather both, to keep up other correspondents.

In answer to the first long desperate letter that I had written to my father after Lucia's visit, in which I told him, without explaining farther, that an accident had happened to the MS., and begging him to release me from the arrangement made before I left England, I had received a derisive note from him, full of ironical sympathy with my misfortunes, and advising me to settle down to another year's work, with a good grace and a contented spirit.

My appeals on behalf of Lucia and myself he simply ignored.

I tore the letter into atoms and flung them over the balcony, and since then my letters to him had been short notes, out of which I studiously kept my own feelings. There was no one now to whom I could either speak or write a word of personal matters.

An anchorite in a cave of the desert could not have been more shut off from that dear communication with his fellows that a man hardly values till he loses it.

When I had lighted the lamp I sat staring at the loose sheets of the manuscript lying on the side table, noting painfully how far it was from completion, and it was only when I lifted it to the middle table for work that I glanced at the letter again.

As my eyes fell on the superscription the blood leapt into my face - it was Howard's. There was a strong disinclination in me to take up the letter, to read it, to let my thoughts flow in his direction at all. Resolutely I had tried to banish the memory of him from my mind, to utterly throw out his image from my recollection. The thought of him was disagreeable, and therefore never welcomed.

The idea of one person cherishing, as the phrase is, hatred, envy, or anger against another, always seems to me incomprehensible. All these are unpleasant sensations, and I sweep them out of my mind as quickly as I possibly can, not from any exalted motives, but simply as useless, cumbering lumber, for which I decline to use my brain at a storehouse. Howard had injured me enough.

Was I to waste my time and my energies in hating him? And

yet the time had not come when I could think of him with calm indifference. Therefore, to scout the idea of him whenever it presented itself, to refuse to dwell upon him and what he had inflicted on me, was the only way to escape additional pain and discomfort for myself. And now, at sight of his handwriting, the beast, the monster of declining hate rose in me again, and I remembered him.

It came back upon me that evening, his image, and I knew that I hated him still. I took up the letter with a feeling of revolt and disgust, as if it had been a filthy object, broke it open, and read: -

"DEAR VICTOR, - I expect you will say to yourself it is the greatest cheek my writing to you, and I know it is, but I am reduced to that state of desperation when a man ceases to feel degradation."

"I am writing to ask you for help - you will wonder how I can. So do I. I wonder at myself. But I know you are the best of fellows, and I feel you will help me now in spite of all that has happened. Victor send me what you can, as near 15 Pounds Sterling as possible, to save me from irrevocable disgrace. I have no one but yourself to apply to. If you refuse I am done for. You will know what a desperate position I am in, I must be in, to ask you at all. -

Yours in despair and everlasting regret,

HOWARD."

I read it through, and then dropped the letter and its envelope into the fire, glad to get rid of the sight of the familiar hand. And I watched it burn, and I thought of the manuscript which must have curled and writhed in the same way, leaf by leaf, as he lighted it, and I asked myself again - What is forgiveness?

I knew that I hated him. I had now the opportunity of consigning him to "irrevocable disgrace," as he put it. But I knew that I should send him the help he asked for on the same principle as I had refrained from injuring him, forgiven him, shaken hands with him. And why? I wondered. What was my motive? Simply, I think, a mere instinct to preserve my own self-respect.

I enclosed a cheque for 20 Pounds Sterling in a blank sheet of paper, put it in an envelope, and went out that same night and posted it. When I had his letter of thanks I glanced through it hastily and then burnt it, and tried to stamp out the re-awakened memory of him from my brain. Weeks followed weeks of the same colourless, monotonous existence; some of them were wasted in physical ill-health, some in mental inactivity, but slowly a manuscript grew and grew again into being.

The slow winter wore away, and the ice froze or the fog pressed on the long French windows of my room. My father invited me to run over and spend Christmas with him, but I dreaded the interruption and the delay in the work. I stayed and pressed forward with it, and in the last days of March the whole book stood complete.

It was one of the first nights of May. The first warm, spring-like night of the season, and the seats at the Concert des Ambassadeurs were crowded by the Parisians consuming their brandied cherries under the canopy of fluttering light green leaves of the opening limes. I sat, one of the audience, and heard the band clashing, and watched the dancers flit on and off the glittering diminutive stage, with indifferent eyes and ears.

I was thinking of my success. The band might thunder its hardest, but it could not drown the publisher's voice in my ears, which repeated over and over the words I had heard that morning. "Yes, M'sieur, your book has been accepted. We shall hope to bring it out in September."

I sat there at peace with all the world. Howard was entirely forgiven now; my father's treatment forgotten. Let the past go.

What did anything matter? And I tapped my stick on the flooring at the end of the songs I had barely heard, out of sheer good humour, and swallowed the second-rate brandy and smoked an infamous cigar with imperturbable complacence; and as I got up with the mass at the finale I heard my nearest neighbour's remark to his companion, which might be freely translated thus:

"How jolly these pigs of English always look!"

As I was leaving, a woman ran down the gravel walk after me, and slipped her arm through mine. I turned and paused. She was very small, pretty, and Parisian from her black eyebrows, cocked like one of her own circumflex accents, to her patent shoes under her silk skirt.

"What do you want" I said, in her own tongue, of course. "Money?"

"We don't put it like that!" she said, thrusting out her red lips.

"Well, it comes to that in the end generally," I said, whirling my cane round in my hand and smiling." It will save you trouble if you take it now," and I offered her two five-franc pieces and withdrew my arm. "Go to the bar and drink my health with it!" She took the money, but still looked at me.

"Give me a kiss!" she said in a low tone, so low that I did not catch the last word.

"Give you what" I asked.

She stamped her foot.

"Un baiser!" she said, with a little French scream. "Embrasse moi! Stupide!"

I laughed slightly as I looked down upon her. It seemed so ludicrous, the proposition, just then to me. I had hardly lived the life I had in Paris for the last thirty months, to now, in the moment of success and freedom, mar its remembrance by even so much as a chance kiss to a cafe chantant girl.

For a second we looked at each other. I noted the tint and the curl of the offered lips, damp with cosmetic, and suggestive of past kisses, and the untouched lips of Lucia seemed almost against my own as I looked. Then I loosened her hand, which clung to my sleeve, and turned from her, and went on down the path. She shrieked some vile French words after me, and sent the five-franc piece rolling after me down the gravel slope.

I laughed and shrugged my shoulders without looking back, and went on out of the gardens down into the now silent streets. What a flood of good spirits poured through my frame as I passed on! I hardly seemed to walk. The buoyant, almost intolerable, unbearable sense of elation within me seemed pressing me forward without volition.

The incident just passed, the woman's hand on mine, the woman's words, though from her they were nothing to me, had yet touched and unlocked those impulses which, until now, had been so sternly repressed, barred down, sepulchred and sealed. They rose upwards, and with an exultant triumph I remembered I was free now to live and to love. My work was done, honourably and faithfully accomplished.

Thirty months lay behind me, an unblemished scroll in time, recording one unbroken stretch of labour, suffering, and repression. And now it was over, and I was at liberty. An unspeakable animation swelled in me; and through all the excited, burning frame seemed to run living fire that formed one thought in my brain, one loved word on my lips - Lucia! Like two planets, at the end of each dark street I turned, I seemed to see her eyes. To her, to her my feet seemed carrying me. I was only returning to my empty room, but no matter! A few days more and then England and Lucia!

I was glad now of everything I had suffered, every emotion

repressed, every weakness vanquished. Strange, wonderful power that lies in that slight, grey tissue which we call brain! It seemed hardly credible that this buoyant sense of exultation, this overflowing, stupendous joy of gratified pride and ambition, this triumphant pleasure in my own powers and their recognition at last, these brilliant vistas that opened in my thoughts, could come from the movements of a little matter with a little blood flowing through it. And yet, so soon, a few years and I, who seemed now like some eternal being carried through worlds of space and endless cycles of years, should be - nothing. Well, no matter; I lived now and Lucia lived!

The street was quite empty, and, half unconsciously, I began to sing the song Bella Napoli, always a favourite of mine, for the sake of the refrain, Santa Lucia! Santa Lucia! The notes echoed down the silent street as the words flowed from my tongue in the intoxication of pleasure - pure, simple, single, undiluted pleasure of the relief after those weary months of strain. The ground beneath my feet seemed buoyant air, each pulse within me beat with keen life, and the name of the woman I loved formed itself again and again on my lips, fluttered and lingered there, almost like the touch of a pure and invisible kiss.

CHAPTER VI

The lamps burned in a subdued way under their dark, rose-coloured shades, the trail of the women's skirts hardly made any sound on the thick carpet, the room was large, and the piano that was being played mildly at the other end of it failed to disturb our conversation.

"Well, now, then?"

I leant over the back of Lucia's low easy-chair and waited eagerly for her answer. It was the second night after my return to England. I had dined with the Grants, and now in this dim, secluded corner of the drawing-room I had the first opportunity of serious conversation with her.

"I don't know, Victor; not at present."

"Lucia! what do you mean!"

"What I say, dearest," she answered quietly.

Looking down on her I could see, beneath a confusion of black eyelashes and dark eyebrow, that the blue eyes looked straight out in front of her, her arm lay along the wicker side-rest of the chair, languid, indolent, relaxed.

"But why?" I said. "Why not at once? Tell me."

She was silent for some time, then she said, -

"When I came to you last year I urged our marriage, and you said it could not be; now you urge it, and I say it cannot be. That's all."

I bit my lips suddenly, and I was glad she was not looking at me. I was silent, too, for a minute; then I said, -

"But surely you are not thinking of punishing me for that; of avenging yourself? You knew all the circumstances, and you acquiesced in my decision. You would not now think of revenge - it is so unlike you!"

"Oh no, no! You misunderstood me. How can you think I should occupy myself with a ridiculous, petty idea of revenge?" and she laughed a slight, fatigued laugh. "No, I merely meant that Chance had so arranged it."

"But how, then? There is no obstacle now."

"Not on your side; no."

"Then what is it, dearest, on yours?"

She did not answer me for a long time, and then it was seemingly with reluctance, and a slight flush crept into her pale face as she said merely the two words, -

"My health."

I hardly know exactly what sensation her answer roused in me, but I think it was nearer relief than any other. In those few seconds of silence all sorts of apprehensions and fears had crowded in upon me. Her health! What barrier need that make between us? And in that moment of selfish passion that was all I heeded.

"What has that to do with our marriage?" I asked, laughing, and bending down farther over her. "You don't mean that you are too ill to go through the ceremony. Come!"

She met my gaze fully, and then laughed too. After a second she said, -

"If you disbelieve me and think I am making up, you can at any rate tell from my looks that I am ill - any man can see that."

I looked at her critically now, remembering my feeling of shock when I had first seen her on my return. Yes; I remembered I had thought her looking fearfully overworked and exhausted, and now I looked at her again with redoubled anxiety.

From the black lace of her dinner dress, cut as low as vanity dared to dictate, and with but one narrow black strip supporting it on her shoulders, her white throat and breast and light head rose like dawn out of the night ocean. The milky arms that lay idly along the chair were as smooth, as downy, but far less dimpled than when I had seen them in Paris. Round the throat I could trace now the clavicles, formerly invisible, and lower, at the edge of her bodice, the depression in the centre of the soft breast was wider. Yes; she was very much thinner, and the face above only confirmed the impression of illness. It was pale, and looked slightly swollen; the eyes were dilated and surrounded with blue shades; the lips were red, almost unnaturally so, to the point of soreness, as they get to look in fever.

"Well, have you come to your conclusion?" she said, as she raised her eyes suddenly and intercepted mine surveying her.

I coloured slightly, looked away, and then said merely, "Yes, you don't look well."

She gave a little slighting laugh, as much as to say, "You might have arrived at that before, one would think!"

"But Lucia," I said, entreatingly, "this is all very serious; do tell me what is wrong."

"Ah, my health becomes a serious matter," she answered, leaning her soft head back on my arm that was resting on the top of her chair, and looking up at me with her brilliant, clever eyes ablaze with indulgent derision, "if it is likely to stop our marriage when YOU desire it!"

I winced before the delicate thrust in her words, and hardly knew whether the pain of them was drowned in the pleasure the confident touch of her head transfused through my arm.

"That is unnecessarily unkind," I answered, quietly. "Your health or ill-health would always be a serious matter, but since you hint it - yes, I admit - if it prevented our marriage, if it came between us now, Lucia, it would surpass even the importance it has at all other times. Tell me what is the matter," I persisted.

The little head turned restlessly on my coat sleeve, and the warmth from the cheeks and lips came into my wrist. She seemed half inclined to yawn, and the delicate left hand, with my ring flashing on it, came to her lips and closed them when they had barely parted.

"People call it hysteria," she said at last. "It is a form of hysteria now, but it did not begin with that. It was overstrain, nervous breakdown, a collapse of the system. See my hand when I hold it up, how it shakes? I can't control that, and my heart beats wildly at the slightest exertion. I am exhausted, limp, Victor, ironed out by the events of last year, very much like what your collar would be without its starch!"

She was looking up at me now and half laughing. She had raised her hand between me and the nearest lamp; it quivered violently, as she said, and looked transparent and scarlet close against the light. I caught it in mine and drew it up to my lips.

"Victor!" she said, indignantly, "release it! remember where we are!"

"I don't care where we are!" I muttered, letting go her hand, but not before I had kissed it passionately across the tiny knuckles and in the palm. It fell nerveless into her lap; her face grew so desperately pallid, even her lips, that I was startled.

"Lucia! What is the matter?"

The lids that seemed ready to sink over her eyes lifted again.

"Nothing; but - I was telling you, just this minute, I am exhausted - done for."

I looked at her in dismay, and I saw her heart must be beating violently; the red geraniums against her breast rose and sank in a series of rapid, irregular jerks.

"I am sorry," I murmured. "Forgive me;" and my heart sank suddenly with a vague, in definable sense of apprehension as I looked at her.

Where was the girl who had come to me a year ago, full of overflowing, eager, exuberant health and life, hungry for love, longing and ardent for a kiss? Not here; somewhere in the past that I had neglected and refused. And the contrast between the two images struck me like a lash across the brain. The next minute I had recovered myself. This was only a passing in disposition of Lucia's, the sooner we were married now the better.

"Well, dearest, if it is only hysteria and nervous strain, and so on," I said, taking up the main thread of our conversation, "then, for that, our marriage and a long rest, in which you would do nothing but amuse yourself, would be the best thing. Make up your mind, Lucia, to give yourself, trust yourself, to me, and I will promise to get you quite well, sooner than any doctor can. I suppose you have seen one?"

"Yes."

"Well, what does he do for you?"

"Oh, I take hydrochloric acid, sulphuric acid, and strychnine through the day, and digitalis and potassium bromide at night."

"Good heavens! Lucia! how can you be so foolish?" I exclaimed. "It's most unwise to take all these things."

"You are not a doctor," she answered languidly.

"No; and therefore I can talk common sense," I said, flushing. "Come, dearest, let us settle which is to be the happiest day in my life."

"Don't fuss, Victor. I can't settle any time just now."

"But at least give me an idea!"

"I can't give you what I have not got myself."

"Do you mean you have no idea when we shall be married?"

"Yes. I have just said so."

My hand closed involuntarily on the back of the chair till the basket-work creaked. She heard it, and felt perhaps, also, the sudden tension in the arm beneath her head. She raised her eyes with a gleam of the old desire in them: they were soft, and her voice was gentle, with out any mockery in it now, as she said, -

"I am excessively sorry about it, Victor, but you may trust me. I will give you some certain date the moment I can, when I am better. You can't think I would voluntarily defer it, do you?"

The whole lovely, inert form heaved a little as she spoke; the eyelids and nostrils in the up-turned face quivered, the lips parted, and, convinced, I bent over her with a hurried, desperate murmur.

"No! no! But, then, when? How long? Is it days, weeks, or the end of the season?"

"Yes; I should think about the end. I can not fix it nearer. It is bad taste to press me any farther."

She lifted her head from my arm and sat up right, though even then, after a minute, her figure drooped languidly towards the side of the chair, and she doubled one of her white, round arms on the wicker-work to form a support. I stood silent, irritated, disappointed, perplexed, biting my lips in nervous, absent-mindedness. She spoke twice to me without my hearing what her words were, and I had to apologise.

"I was only saying I should like you to see the "Death of Hyacinthus" now it is finished: see the result of last year's efforts and the cause of this year's ill-health!"

"Certainly; I want to see it very much. When may I?"

"To-morrow, if you like, but I want you to see the Academy first. I should like you to come to it prejudiced, with your eyes full of all the successful pictures of the year."

"Is it not at the Academy, Lucia?"

"Don't look so apprehensive!" she said, with a slight laugh. "It has not been rejected - simply, I could not get it finished in time for presentation. I was ill, and it just missed this season by a very little."

"And now, what are you going to do with it?"

"I must offer it next year, that's all."

"What a disappointment for you!"

"Yes, I should have thought so some time ago; but I seem to be much more apathetic now to everything. Each year that one lives one gets to expect less and less from life, and one grows more philosophic, more contented with what is thrown in one's way, and less disappointed when one's hopes and expectations are not realised. Judging by those things which we do gain and enjoy and experience the worth lessness of, I suppose we learn by degrees to infer that others so longed-for and coveted would prove as valueless if possessed."

Her voice was low and tired, and had the sound of suppressed tears in it.

"You are in a depressed frame of mind," I said.

"Yes;" then, with a cynical smile, "hysteric, as I told you. Well, will you come to-morrow about eleven, and then afterwards we can come back here to criticise 'Hyacinthus'?"

"Yes; I shall be delighted."

"I think mama is going to take our carriage, so come in yours, will you?"

"Very good," I answered, and there was a long silence. Not broken, in fact, until there was the stir of some of the guests leaving.

As the third or fourth left the room, I came round and took her hand as I stood in front of her.

"Good-night, Lucia, I hope you may be granted all the sleep you have stolen from me," I said gently; then, partly influenced by the contact of that delicious hand, and prompted by my own impulse, and partly deliberately to excite, if possible, her own instincts as allies to fight for me, I pressed it hard as I added, -

"On how many more nights is this hated formula,

'Good-night,' to be said between us? Minimise them, my darling, for my sake!"

Into the tone I allowed to enter all the strength of my feelings at the moment. She only coloured painfully up to the heavy eyes, whether from confusion or pleasure or passion I could not tell. She made no answer, and the soft, captive hand struggled faintly to be free.

We were surrounded the next instant by the press of talking, laughing guests passing down to the door, and I could do nothing but drop her hand and leave her with a composed face, and my brain feeling literally on fire. The perplexity, mystery, uncertainty, and irritation which Lucia's illness and manner had poured suddenly in upon the elation, the assured triumph, the excited expectations and eager desire with which I had come, produced a state of thought in which I hardly recognised my reasoning being.

I made my way over to Mrs. Grant with the conventional smile, and then, once without the drawing-room, hurried down to the door and the night air. In the hall I recognised, standing waiting for his carriage, a familiar figure. It was a man I had known intimately in India: he was home now on furlough, and as friends we were often invited to the same houses.

"I say, Dick," I said, as I came up to him, "it's a lovely night. Are you game for a walk? If so, send the carriage home and come with me round to my place. I want your advice and condolences."

We were at the foot of the stairs. The other men and women had collected nearer the door.

"Condolences! Why, yesterday you told me congratulations were the order of the day!" he answered in a tone of good-natured raillery.

"They are so no longer," I answered, gloomily. "My head is simply splitting too. I can't think where I get these confounded headaches," I muttered, pushing the hair up off my forehead, and wishing I could push off some of the oppressing ideas. "Are you coming with me, Dick?"

He looked at me attentively, and possibly seeing the excitement I tried to suppress, and the flush it drove to my face, he debated my sobriety. I think he came to the right conclusion, for the next moment he said, -

"Yes; I'll come. Just let me get my over coat and tell the coachman."

I had the same thing to do, and we met a second or two later at the bottom of the steps, and turned to walk towards my place. As we walked down the street he slipped his arm in mine and said, -

"You seem frightfully upset. What has happened?"

"That's just what I want to know!" I answered. "If I knew I should not so much mind, but this is what I hate about women, they never will speak out nor come to the point. It is the one great fault of the sex. I despise it utterly. It can do no good, and it is most annoying and irritating to a person who has a right to confidence."

"My dear fellow," he said, soothingly, "you can't expect your fiancee, if that's what you mean, to be so uncommonly direct in speech as you are! You have a way of very much going to the point in everything, but you won't find it in other people, even throwing women out of the question."

"What is the use of wrapping things up in mystery? But women delight in it! The more they can mystify and mislead and perplex you, and leave their real or their possible meaning doubtful and involved, the greater the pleasure they have. They will carry on a conversation for hours by hints, suggestions, ambiguous terms, allusions, phrases that may mean anything or nothing, and then leave at the end, in obscurity, the whole matter, which could have been explained and made perfectly clear and settled on a satisfactory basis in a few short sentences. It's a petty, abominable trait in their character."

Dick raised his eyebrows considerably.

"She has offended, evidently," he said.

"Offended? She simply tortured me all this evening, either intentionally or involuntarily. She said too little and too much. And her manner was worse than her words. I could not make out whether she was telling me the truth or a series of delicate excuses; she herself did not calculate on my believing. Everything she said to-night, if proved false, she might justify to-morrow by saying, 'Oh, well, of course, I never thought you would take that seriously; I thought you would understand that was a euphemism to save your feelings, and so on; you know one does not say to a person's face one is tired of him and wishes the thing off.' That is what she may say afterwards, or, of course, what she told me may be the truth. It may be an excuse that sounds like the truth, or the truth that sounds like an excuse. She contrived to leave it confoundedly indistinct, and that is what I complain of."

"You haven't given me any clue yet as to what the conversation was," Dick said quietly as we paced down the silent street.

My head seemed reeling with pain and the blood that flowed to it. The moonlight, and the black shadows it deepened, jumped together before my eyes.

"The accursed upshot of it was that she won't have anything to do with our marriage at present," I returned.

"Oh! And what reason did she assign?"

"After considerable hesitation she said her health; but, as I say, she would not speak out, and such an excuse between us is monstrous!"

"After considerable hesitation she said her health; but, as I say, she would not speak out, and such an excuse between us is monstrous! Ours is not a formal 'mariage de convenance;' it lies with ourselves. She is obviously not seriously ill; if she hesitates on her own account she must know she has nothing to fear from me; if she hesitates on mine, then it is folly and nonsense. I don't care about anything! I don't care what is the matter with her, I would marry her if she were dying, rotting of leprosy to-morrow!"

"I say, old fellow, you must not excite yourself like this! You will be seriously ill if you don't look out," Dick answered, remonstratingly. "It's no use working yourself up into a fever."

"I am not working myself up; unfortunately that has been done for me," I answered, with a short laugh. "Well, Dick, I am sick of everything, disgusted with everything! It's the same old story perpetually repeated. All that one fixes one's eyes on in the distance turns into dust as one approaches it. For the last year I have thought of this meeting this evening, and now it has come, what is it?"

"You are taking me by surprise to-night, Victor! I remember you in the regiment as so deuced calm."

"I'm never calm!" I returned. "Exteriorly, yes, of course, for one's own convenience and self-respect, to outsiders, one is always calm; but the exterior is not the reality. I am not one of those things naturally which I command myself into being: existence to me is nothing but a close-fitting, strangling, self-restraint. It drags upon me like a prisoner's gangrening fetter, and I'm getting tired of it. I think I'll slip it off altogether!"

I talked straight out of the distraction of my own thoughts, the pain in my head was acute, stunning my brain, and my vision seemed all wrong, as when one has been drinking. I was conscious of Dick looking at me anxiously, as he said -

"That's all nonsense! You are quite out of your senses this evening! You wouldn't throw up your life now, when you are just on the point of success, surely?"

"If I can't force our marriage, it's likely to come to that, I think," I muttered. "I am totally at a loss. I know nothing. I can conjecture nothing. I have not seen her nor heard from her this past year; and now she will say nothing. I pressed her as much, I think, as a fellow decently could. If she had spoken clearly and definitely it would have been different. Whatever statement a woman made to me of any painful facts; or if she came to me with any confession of folly, or change of feeling, or misfortune, or whatever it was, no matter what, I should enter into it and understand her. But Lucia to-night treated me like a stranger, fenced with me like an enemy. I have no clue as to what to think and what to believe. Simply, I see that she is no longer keen on the matter, and there is a large possibility of my not having her at all. By God! if it is so" -

I broke off into silence. After all, there is no use in talk; and the knives twisted backwards and forwards in my head helped to stop speech.

We walked on in silence. The streets were very quiet here; we had left the Grants' late, and now it was getting towards morning. We verged directly towards Knightsbridge; for some time our steps were the only sound. Then, after a pause, Dick said quietly -

"I think, Victor, you are going on a wrong tack altogether. You don't make enough allowance for the fact that she is a girl, and has not seen you for a year, remember. It is all very well for you to talk of to-the-point confessions and plain statements, but practically, if a girl were to talk as frankly as you would like, I am afraid the idea of modesty would rather come to grief."

Victoria Cross

"Oh! modesty," I said impatiently, "be - Modesty! It's all very well as a pretty, becoming, every-day fashion, but it should be laid aside in the serious matters of life. It is an artificiality; admirable, useful, excellent as a daily conventional rule, but it should yield when there is a great natural question at issue. Modesty! a fictitious, artificial, inculcated shame to intrude itself between two people considering gravely the vital matter of their love, their union, their future life! It's preposterous!"

"It very often does so," remarked Dick. "I am not saying whether it should or it shouldn't."

"No," I answered more calmly; "and I entirely see what you mean, and I think you are perfectly right there. Lucia is steeped in fashion, soaked through with the prejudice and bringing up of her own rank. And I suppose I do like it and expect it, certainly, as a general rule; only, when the thing on hand is very important, and a society woman fences with you behind a screen of elegant, delicate language, you feel some-times you would prefer the intelligible candour of a kitchen maid."

Dick laughed.

"I doubt the charm of the latter individual, Vic! You must have a little more patience with this girl, and the confidence will come by degrees, if you don't lose your self-command with her; but I'd advise you to be careful. The way in which you have been talking to me now gives an impression of - well, almost brutality, that I didn't think was in you."

I laughed contemptuously.

"Oh, you needn't be afraid of the word; I know there is a lot of it in me. It's just that knowledge that enables me to keep it under. I know if I had not kept myself, for the sake of the work, out of it, that I should have led a brutish existence. However, you needn't think that I am going to frighten Lucia. I have had such a deuce of a lot of practice in patience and restraint, and all those fine things, that I am quite sure of myself when I am with her. But as to gaining her confidence, that is impossible before the ceremony, I believe. She has been brought up in that monstrous idea, like the rest of our fashionable girls, that the man into whose possession she is to give herself utterly with the ceremony, up to the last moment before it, is to be treated with the most absolute reserve. The contrast is too ludicrous - driven to the point of exaggeration to which they drive it. In Lucia's eyes an unusual, an unfashionable word, no matter how great the necessity for it, is a crime. I believe she would walk to the block rather than let a word pass her lips in my hearing an hour before our marriage that in twenty-four hours afterwards might be a common phrase between us. You may call it modesty and charming, if you like. All I can say is, there are limits to its charm."

The approach of morning was distinct now. A grey light hung in a faint misty veil over the Green Park and top of Piccadilly. As it fell from the cloudy, neutral-tinted sky, it showed one solitary figure, a woman with a trailing skirt and battered hat, passing Hyde Park corner.

In the waste of deserted street and roadway, glimmering in the dull, grey light, that one dishevelled black figure reminded one of the remnant of some wrecked vessel, drifting at dawn along a sullen coast. She drifted somewhat faster up to us as we came to the corner and touched Dick, who was next to the road, on the arm. He shook her hand off without speaking.

"Have you any money with you, Dick?" I asked.

"Yes; but I am not going to give any to her," he answered.

I would have given the woman some, but I had none. I had left it behind when I changed my clothes for dinner. She heard Dick's answer to me plainly, and it exasperated her. All the natural, florid, unstudied eloquence of the lower orders was at her command, and well-turned periods of perfect abuse and neat incisive remarks upon our characters, our persons and attributes generally, rippled in a smooth, unbroken stream from her lips as she followed us. Just at that moment there was not a policeman nor any other being within sight.

We walked on, and the woman's curses and imprecations upon us filled the grey silence of the street. At last a porter on his way to work passed us, and she transferred her attentions and oratory to him. Dick glanced at me and laughed.

"Well, there was an extensive vocabulary, Victor! How would some of those words sound in your fiancee's mouth?"

I laughed too.

"You always were good at a sophistical sneer, but vile language has nothing to do with what I was talking about."

"No; of course not. It does strike one as curious, doesn't it," he added after a minute, "that a creature like that and the girl we have been with this evening can belong to the same sex."

"Well, I don't know," I answered; "I know there is the sort of idea that it is funny, but somehow it does not strike me more with reference to woman than to ourselves. I mean it does not seem more incongruous than that a man like yourself and an offal sweeper belong to the same sex."

"No; perhaps not. One of those houses is yours, isn't it?" Dick said.

"Yes; number 2," I answered, as we went up to the door.

"They seem to have turned the light out."

I opened the door and Dick went in. I followed, and when the door was shut behind us the hall was in nether darkness. We found our way to the foot of the stairs, where an undefined heap barred our way. Not knowing what it was I kicked it, and Dick exclaimed, -

"Take care! I think that's your man," and a groan confirmed the statement.

"Hullo, Walters! I am very sorry. I had no idea it was you. I hope I haven't hurt you!" I said as the servant got on his feet. "Why do you turn the lights out? However, it's just as well you are here. Bring me upstairs the soda, champagne, and the new lot of cigars. I suppose there is the lamp in my room?"

"Yes, sir."

"You won't care to turn out again, Dick, to-night, will you?" I said as we went upstairs. "There's an awfully comfortable sofa in my room, quite as good as a bed. Will you accept that?"

"Oh yes; I always find I can go to sleep anywhere. Do you remember, when we were camping out at Shikarpur, those nights on the shaky-legged native benches?"

"Rather! That was when I never bothered about anything. I have never slept so well since."

We went into my room. Two lamps were burning here, and the thick blinds shut out all signs of the dreary dawning light. Walters followed us in a few seconds and set a tray of glasses and bottles on the table. I flung off my overcoat and sat down in an arm-chair, pressing the palms of my hands hard on my forehead in the vain effort to deaden the tearing pain.

"Try some of those cigars," I said, after a minute, "they are not bad, and take whatever you like to drink," and I got up and filled my glass at the same time.

"I think that brandy is the worst thing for your head," remarked Dick, looking dubiously at the glass.

"But I am so confoundedly thirsty!"

"Take the soda without the brandy, then. Really, I would

advise you not to touch that spirit to-night."

"Oh, I don't much care! let it be the soda;" and I filled another tumbler with the latter and drank it. "But what is your own opinion about this business with Lucia," I asked, when Dick had stretched himself on the sofa and started his cigar. "What puzzles me so is the great change in her - a change apparently in the whole tenour of her feelings. You can't think how wide the difference is between her now and a year ago. I told you that she came over to Paris to see me, didn't I?"

Dick nodded.

"That was only twelve months back, and she was simply - well, she was evidently very much in love then. You know what I mean, and she made no effort to conceal it. She urged our marriage; and then, when we decided it was impossible, she would have liked me to go any reasonable lengths in demonstration of my love for her, and so on. I made a mistake there, perhaps, but I thought it unwise. We hardly knew where we were as it was. She seemed utterly weak, and I felt she might say things in those moments she would be fearfully cut up to remember afterwards. It seemed dishonourable in my shackled, circumscribed position to lead her any farther on. That was my idea - perhaps it was mistaken - I don't know. Anyway we shook hands merely. Then, at that time, she invited a kiss in every way short of demanding it. Now, to-night I kissed her hand, not a very extraordinary nor embarrassing action, and yet I thought she was going to faint as a result. It moved some very strong sensation, repulsion or disgust, or something, and I want to know what."

"You see, Vic," Dick said, after a minute or two of silence, laying down the cigar and driving his elbow into the sofa cushion, and leaning his head on his hand. He looked past me absently towards the fender, and spoke as a person does whose opinion has long since been formed. "We can't hold over anything in this life, opportunities, our own powers, health, youth, they are all things you can't store for the future. All we can do is to use them when they are put into our hands. Still less can we reserve and warehouse our own feelings and emotions, and least of all, those of others. You might compare passion to a gas. If you allow gas its expansion it diffuses itself and is lost. If you subject it to confinement with close pressure, it becomes a liquid and loses its original form. It is the same with passion. It is impossible to maintain it as such. Either it evaporates in gratification or it undergoes some metamorphosis in suppression."

I said nothing. There was a sort of coldness and weight in his words and tone that increased my own apprehensions.

"You can keep nothing up to the pitch of a crisis. We all know that. Even a kettle of water, when it is once boiling, you cannot keep it so. It must boil over into the flames or simmer down or dry up. And if you reject a woman at the crisis of her passion, there is an enormous probability that, in waiting, her virtue or her inclination or her health will break down. Either her feelings may transport her into some folly or they may cool. If her will is too strong to allow the folly, and her nature too ardent to permit the cooling, then her constitution must give way. This last is what, judging from all I see, I should think - since you ask my opinion, old fellow, you know - has happened in Lucia's case."

I looked at him with a faint feeling of surprise. His manner, voice, and words conveyed such an idea of certainty and perfect decision in his own mind.

"Yes," I answered; "I suppose that is it. Well, that is what she told me, virtually, herself."

"You cannot wonder at it!"

I coloured hotly as I answered, -

"I know it seems as if I had been a confounded prig in refusing her last year - people may say so; but if I had given in and kept her with me in Paris, then everybody would have been slanging me for that!"

Dick laughed.

"No, Victor; I am not slanging you for one or the other course. You acted up to your own principle - every fellow must do that; but I am not sure your principle is the best - that perpetual denial to impulse, that refusal to take what you can get in the moment, because of what you may be called upon to pay hereafter. At any rate, it may not be the luckiest nor the happiest. But still, in the case of a man who has many equally strong wishes, it is difficult to say what he should do. In your case the upshot of either resolution would have been the same - as things are, you will get your book out and be discontented; in the other case, you would have married Lucia and been discontented!"

"You may be as cynical as you please," I muttered, with my hands pressed over my eyes. "I am not responsible for the complex nature of the human brain, nor can I simplify it. I know what I am going to do now. Having secured the work, I am going to gain Lucia too, if it is in the power of any man - whether, as you put it, her virtue, or her health, or her inclination, or the whole lot together, have broken down!"

"And if you don't get her, you will get over it: we all do, Vic," he said, with a smile.

"Very possibly," I assented.

It was not worth while to discuss a contingency I had determined to prevent.

"A man's profession is his best friend," Dick went on, stretching himself out on the couch. "That he can command; and for the rest - purchasable pleasures - those he can command. These affaires-de-coeur, which you can't command, are always more bother than they are worth."

There was silence, then he added, -

"One good one, though, fairly early in life, is useful, like vaccination. You are not so likely to fall in love again after it; just as, after vaccination, you are not so likely to have smallpox. For myself, I should prefer smallpox to being in love."

I merely laughed, without replying. In my present state I was not sure that he was far wrong.

"I say," Dick remarked, after a pause; "you are looking most awfully seedy. Hadn't you better turn in and try and get some sleep? One always thinks one can't, but one generally does."

"Yes; I think I had better," I said, getting up. I turned one lamp out and the other down.

"It's odd - I wonder what the ultimate, future event will be" -

"'Quid sit futurum eras, fuge quaerere,'" answered Dick, with a laugh, as he turned and settled himself on the couch.

"There are a couple of rugs," I said, depositing them on his feet. "Draw them up if you're cold."

"All right. Thanks! Good-night!"

"Good night!"

I slipped off my clothes and got into bed, feeling almost uncertain on my feet. My head seemed literally whirling and swimming in pain. When I awoke the following morning and looked round it was past ten. Dick had gone. I looked at the couch, it was empty, and a note was stuck by his pin into the sofa pillow. I sat up in bed, and by leaning forward and extending my arm I got hold of the pillow, and thence the paper and read it.

"8 A.M. - You are still asleep and I don't like to wake you, but I want to be back at my place by nine, so I am departing like the guest of an Arab. If you have nothing better to do this evening, come and dine with me. Army and Navy. Seven."

"Very good," I thought; I put the note and the pin on the table beside me, and got up. The headache was gone, and the head felt none the worse for it. The sun was streaming in through the blinds now. The gloom, the apprehensions, the pain of the previous night, had all cleared from the field together. I dressed and shaved with a steady hand, thinking, in a sane, easy way, very different from the inflamed, convulsive working of the brain last night. The work was set afloat in Paris - I should soon find readers on the asphalt - that quarter of my sky was clear. As for the sudden darkening squall that had sprung up in the other quarter, formerly so serene, the quarter over which reigned Lucia's star - it was only a squall, it would pass. She must be capable of being roused again to those feelings she had once known. And if I had nothing else, I had, at least, in my favour the sheer force and intensity of my own passion - which is, after all, the weapon under which a woman quickest sinks. I felt that I cared more keenly for Lucia than most men of eight-and-twenty in the nineteenth century care for the women they marry. I was conscious of it instinctively; even if the memory of these last ten barren, empty years that I had lived did not convince me that a passion for any one object would be greater in myself than in men whose multiplicity of previous loves must lessen the value of each succeeding one. My work, which had been Lucia's successful rival, had protected her from lesser ones.

Nothing, except the possession of this woman, had ever been a synonym of pleasure with me, and therefore its expectation had a stronger hold over me than it could have had over a man who was accustomed to acknowledge and recognise pleasure under a hundred names. I felt the impetus of this undiffused, undissipated passion, in its undivided strength, stir and vitalise all my energies, and its power over my own frame made me involuntarily, instinctively confident of the power it would have over hers.

"We will see how long it is before you capitulate, oh my fortified and arrogant city!" I thought, as I finished dressing and went downstairs. My father was reading the paper, apparently waiting breakfast for me. We were on the very best of terms now.

He felt convinced of my capability to work, and assured of my success. With that surprising tendency of the human mind to delegate its own powers to another, he accepted completely the verdict of the Parisian publisher upon qualities he had had under his own observation for an odd twenty years. Now, forsooth, because another man had told him so, he took it for granted that I had some talent. And all the time we had lived together he had hesitated to form that opinion from first-hand knowledge. Extraordinary trait in human nature, this liking to be thought for, instead of thinking for yourself! This waiting to take up, second-hand, ready-made, the views of another man, even when the fresh materials are at your hand, and you may examine them and form your own. It is a universal tendency, of course, and displays itself everywhere; in religion, in morality, in fashions, in vices, in simple conversation - everywhere.

The glorious and free gift of Nature to every man, the capacity for perception and judgment, he shamefacedly, as if it were a disgrace, tries to shift off upon another. It always amuses me immensely when brought before me, and it did now in my father's case. He assumed, as innumerable people do, that success or failure proves or disproves merit, which is such a curious opinion, as remarkable as if a person believed the absence or presence of the hall-mark proved or disproved the identity of gold. On no point did he and I differ more widely than on this.

It has always seemed to me that the formation of a judgment and opinion is an involuntary function of the mind, not a matter of effort, as others seem to regard it. Your judgment may be wrong, so may your opinion; your perception may be misled. I understand that. But can you exist without judgment, without opinion, without perception, till another man hand you his? This is hard to realise.

My father in all these years had not said my son is a fool and will not succeed, nor had he said my son is clever and will succeed, but what he had said was this, he may be a fool or he may be clever, we will see what the publishers say. And this attitude of mind, which repeated itself in different forms in half the men one meets, is fascinatingly incomprehensible to me. If I have the opportunity of seeing a man or testing a ring, what do I care, what does it matter to me, whether he is successful or unsuccessful, whether the ring is hall-marked or not! I have my own eyes, ears, and intelligence at command. What more do I want? Give me the man or the metal: in a very short time I have decided their worth to my own satisfaction. I may be wrong in my estimate, of course, but that is another matter.

If my brain is in a healthy state, I can do more avoid its forming an exact, personal opinion of the man, and a computation of his powers, than I can avoid my eye spontaneously taking his shape and muscles into its vision. In their natural, unimpaired state, neither organ should need artificial aid. But my father was looking at me now through the mental spectacles of my success, which made to him hugely big that merit which, before, he could not see at all. Thanks to those spectacles, an easy indulgence was granted me. Little that I could do now was wrong. Another man had thought fit to pay me for my powers. That elevated me in his estimation as the powers themselves never had done. He had no longer any wish apparently to oppose me. Since my brains were now authenticated by the seal of a publisher, he was sufficiently satisfied that they might be trusted to decide my own life and conduct. However, besides all this, he was strictly a man of his word, and having promised that, with my success, all opposition to my marriage would cease, he kept his conditions, as I had kept mine.

"I am very sorry to be so late," I said, as we drew our chairs to the table. "I am afraid you have waited for me."

"My dear boy, a few minutes are of no consequence!"

"I had rather a stiff headache last night, and only got to sleep when it was nearly time to get up. I hope I didn't wake you coming home last night? That idiot Walters must needs turn out the gas and go to sleep in the hall. Of course I kicked him over. Did it disturb you?"

"I should think it was calculated to disturb Walters more than me!" he returned. "No; I didn't hear you. Were you late? Will you have sole or bacon?"

"Sole, please," I said. "Yes; Dick and I walked back from Lucia's place."

"How did you find her?" he asked, stirring his tea I had just handed him, and looking at me. "Don't you think she has deteriorated in looks very much?"

"Enormously," I replied, without hesitation.

There is nothing like conceding at once to your opponent any point that you admit yourself. It saves discussion being wasted upon that which you are really agreed about, and gives more weight to all you refuse to relinquish to him afterwards.

My father looked a little surprised, and did not answer immediately, and I continued, -

"She was always, as far as I remember, a girl who could look exceedingly pretty and positively plain, and all the intermediate gradations, within twenty-four hours, but really," I added, meeting his eyes across the breakfast table, and the full blaze of the sunlight falling into my own, "to me, in any one of them, she is equally" -

I hesitated a second, and he put in -

"Attractive?"

It was not the word I should have used, but it served, and I let it pass.

"I suppose it's really her talent that fetches you as much as anything, eh?" he said, after a few minutes.

"And her character," I answered; "her whole personality. I suppose all those things weighed at first, but, as a matter of fact, now it is quite enough that she is the woman I have determined upon."

"An admission of your own obstinacy," he answered, tartly.

"That may be the right term for it," I returned, "but I hardly think it is. Theoretically, Lucia has belonged to me the past four years. An idea, a habit of the mind, is full grown and has some strength at four years of age."

My father said nothing, but lapsed into the silence of defeat or of contempt, and we pursued our breakfast.

"Will you let me have the victoria this morning?" I said, after a long silence. "She wants me to drive her to the Academy."

"Of course; I'm glad you can find something to do here. I'm afraid of its seeming dull to you after Paris."

I looked up with elevated eyebrows.

"And wherein do you imagine the gaiety of Paris consisted?" I asked.

"Oh, I've no doubt you found plenty of amusement there," he answered, with an indulgent smile.

"I assure you there was not one single hour of the whole time that was not spent in work or thought," I said, seriously.

He laughed.

"I am delighted to hear it, I'm sure, Victor," he said, with the air of a person who accepts the general truth of a statement with a large reservation of their own opinion on the details of it. However, I did not care. I had worked for my own sake; lived correctly for my own sake - and whether another knew it or not mattered to me not at all.

"No; on the contrary, I am very pleased to be back," I said. "I always look upon the place where you are as home."

A pleased expression came over his face as I spoke. We were sincerely attached to each other in spite of the jarring dissonance of character. Later that same morning when I was sitting beside Lucia as we drove to the Academy, I studied her closely in the sharp morning light, and I was alarmed at the pallor and exhaustion of her face. I am not an admirer of ill-health in any form. The hectic flush of phthisis, even, dear to the poets, has positively no charm for me; and Lucia's illness was not phthisis, and certainly did not enhance her looks.

"Who is your medical man, Lucia?" I asked.

"Why do you wish to know?"

"That I may be satisfied that he is a good one."

"I should prefer not to tell you his name."

"Why?"

"Because I object," she said simply, in her coldest tone.

"That is not a sufficient reason."

"I am of opinion that it is," she returned frigidly, with a supercilious accent.

I leant back in the carriage without answering, and looked away from her. How I hated her in that moment! After all, I thought, why do you trouble to get this particular woman above everything? Fifty women that you meet in the course of a week are as pretty - possiblyof more worth - probably more civil. Why not select a more accessible divinity? Or else content yourself with Horace's parabilem venerem facilemque?

Then I glanced involuntarily at her, and I knew it was impossible. My eyes swept over the form beside me, as she sat cold, impassive; her attitude one of quiet ease, her whole mien the essence of calm self-possession. That excess of pride and dignity and supercilious arrogance that in Lucia replaced, at times, her seductive plasticity at others, had always exercised a violent attraction over me. And now, when this pride seemed joined with a positive hostility to myself, it failed to repel; it simply raised to its highest pitch a savage and acrimonious determination to subdue it.

As I sat silent, with my eyes turned away from her to the blaze of glaring pavement and roadway, and noted mechanically the crush of traffic on ahead, Dick's remark on my brutality recurred to me, and I forced the most good-natured smile to my lips, and the quietest tone to my voice, as I turned to her and said, -

"Of course, dearest, I will consider it sufficient if you say so."

Perhaps she expected farther opposition, and my yielding surprised her. She looked at me full for a minute in silence, then, failing to discover a trace of the savage irritation I was feeling, she laid her hand impulsively on mine, and said with a smile, -

"You are a dear, good-tempered fellow, Victor!" at which I laughed - considerably.

The Academy is a place of all others, I should think, most calculated to fatigue and oppress a person in nervous ill-health. It was just twelve when Lucia and I arrived. The sun was at its hottest, and the crowds within the rooms at their thickest. The air seemed lifeless and laden with dust, swept up by the women's dresses, and filled with a mixture of scents from White Rose to Eau de Cologne. The daylight was harshly bright, and the unbroken lines of pictures in their glaring gilt frames, annoyed and jarred upon the eye.

We moved very slowly with the rank of people passing down our side of the gallery. Lucia never removed her eyes from the walls, except to glance at me and make me refer to a name in the catalogue, and the women who passed her were able to scrutinise her dress and face without a return glance. This they did to the utmost limits of good breeding, for both were sufficiently worthy of notice.

Whether Lucia looked pretty or plain, at her best or her worst, she always looked more or less striking. Some women are like this; they can appear everything but quiet and common-place. Lucia would be noticed everywhere, sometimes favourably, sometimes the reverse; but noticed she must infallibly be. An exceptionally beautiful figure, a certain extravagance in dress, and an unusually fair skin made her conspicuous where far more regular faces and straight profiles passed unnoticed. She herself was absolutely indifferent to everything save the paintings. Twice I called her attention to men who saluted her without being seen by her as she passed close to them.

"I am very sorry," she said in answer. "It is a stupid fashion to notice one's friends here. One should not be supposed to recognise them at the Academy any more than in church!"

We drifted on slowly with the mass, and at last came to a standstill before a wedge of figures in front of a prominent canvas. A nude female figure stood upright, facing the spectator, with both arms upraised to fasten a pomegranate blossom in the tightly twisted hair: an indefinite heap of sketchy clothing lay upon the ground.

"The title?" murmured Lucia; and I pressed my way a little forward to see the number, looked it up in the catalogue, and read to her "The Toilette." "Before the toilette! I should think," said Lucia, in a satirical whisper. I nodded and laughed.

We could not move on till the circle before us moved, and we stood silent looking at the shadowy representation of human flesh and blood smiling with fixed inanity from the canvas.

"The most successful picture of the year!" remarked one man just in front of us.

"Eminently artistic!" murmured another, stifling a yawn.

"Did you ever see such a thing?" said Lucia. "No living woman ever looked like that!"

"No," I answered, unguardedly.

Lucia threw a sudden, brilliant, mocking glance over my face.

"Come, Victor! you ought to have said you didn't know!"

I coloured, and then laughed.

"Ah, yes; so I ought. Well, really, I answered you in absence of mind."

"Oh, don't apologise! Let's sit down."

I glanced at her face. It was white to the lips which laughed so readily. I looked round desperately. The lounge behind was filled completely before the most successful picture of the year.

"Let us try another room," I said, hastily drawing her arm more through mine. It leant heavily there, and she grew more pallid.

"They are all alike - I can't stand the heat - we must go, I think," she murmured.

"It doesn't seem very easy," I said.

Lucia threw a helpless glance round on the crown pressing up eagerly to catch a glimpse of the popular painting, and some one in artistic circles recognised her.

A whisper went from one to the other of the little sets within the crowd, and they fell back from us; heads were turned from the canvas towards Lucia. There was an exit made, and I walked determinedly through the staring loungers, who yielded before us.

A voice said behind us, -

"They say she'll be the greatest artist of the times!"

"How I envy her!" came a girl's answer.

Lucia's blue-white lips smiled mockingly.

"Take me home, Victor," she said, faintly.

. . . . . .

The hot summer days dragged slowly by.

The Grants did not leave town, and I hesitated to do as my father suggested, and go myself. I waited, and saw Lucia daily, and hoped daily to hear the words I thirsted for, but she persistently refused to say anything of herself or her health or her wishes. I might see her as often as I liked, go and come to and from her house as I pleased, but speak of our marriage or allow me any of the privileges of a fiance she would not.

As the weeks passed the life became intolerable for me. I could not expect my book to be produced till the autumn. There was no fresh impetus in my brain toward writing another. All my thoughts centred now round this woman, whom I saw apparently growing more listless, languid, and indifferent to myself every day.

The nervous strain told upon me. Night followed night in which I got no sleep, and which left me with a blinding headache to commence the day. Gradually these headaches lengthened, till they stretched throughout the tedious, desultory hours; and one stifling August afternoon, lying, dizzy with pain, on the couch, I determined to win an answer from her or cut all the ties, dear and clinging though they might be, and leave her finally.

To-morrow! What was to-morrow? My brain went round when I tried to think of the simplest thing. We had some men coming in to luncheon, I remembered, but I would go and see her early in the morning. We were generally alone with each other in the morning. This evening I should have no chance of speaking as I meant to speak. When the evening came, I felt unfit even to go and see her, and it was later than I intended the next morning when I reached the house. I had made myself later, too, by stopping on the way to get her some flowers. There was little in the shop worth having but some lilies, all price, scent, and brilliance. I took these and hurried on. They were very fine specimens, certainly, I thought, as I glanced overthem. I care very little for flowers; they are useful, of course, sometimes, as a present for women, and a button-hole; but there, for me, their merits cease. Howard would have sentimentalised into two or three verses over these.

I found her in the drawing-room, as usual now, for the studio was rarely ever visited, except when she went to gaze in an abstracted way on the finished work. She was doing nothing - as usual now - she who formerly worked without ceasing every hour of daylight. Nor was there anything near her that suggested or made possible the supposition of work or even occupation. Every book was ranged in different cases in remote corners of the room. Not a newspaper, nor blotting-book, nor pen, lay on the table. She was sitting in an armchair facing the window, her knees crossed idly, her elbow leaning on a table beside her, her head resting on her hand; idle, listless. Perhaps her toilette alone, as an elaborate work, might excuse her from any other for several hours. She looked round with a smile, and even that was tired, as I entered and crossed to her.

"How are you, dearest, to-day?" I said, as I took her hand. "No, pray, don't get up," I added, as she made a movement to rise, and to obviate her doing so, I dropped into a low wicker chair, which I drew up close to hers, and laid the lilies on her lap.

"I am as well as usual, thanks, Victor. These are lovely! Where did you get them?"

"At a shop in Regent Street. I wanted something extraordinary, but they had nothing."

"What could you have more beautiful than these?"

"Beautiful? Yes; but there is no worth in beauty unless there is some peculiarity about it to attract one. May I do that for you?"

She had lifted the flowers and begun to fasten them into the front of her bodice, a difficult work, covered, as it was, with an intricate maze of lace.

"Thank you! I am perfectly capable of achieving it myself."

The familiar, cold pride in the tone brought an ironical smile to my lips - suppressed, however, before she saw it.

"You are afraid of the risk of my hand touching your breast accidentally in fastening a flower!" I thought, satirically, as I watched her in silence, and remembered the mission with which I had come. I glanced at the clock and saw it was later than I thought.

"Do you know what I have come for this morning, Lucia?" I asked, leaning my elbow on the arm of her chair, and looking into the soft blue eyes that seemed to have a sort of timidity in them of me now.

"To torment me as usual, I suppose," she answered.

"That depends upon how you take it," I said, with a slight laugh.

"I have come to say Good-bye."

I watched her keenly as I spoke, and I saw she was perceptibly startled. She fixed her eyes upon me, and the colour began to recede visibly from her face. However, she only said calmly after a moment, -

"Well, if you are going away, I shall have peace at any rate."

"Yes, dear," I answered gently, "you will have peace certainly as far as I am concerned, for if I go now I shall consider our engagement terminated."

Lucia started into an upright position in her chair.

"Victor!" she exclaimed, fixing two widely-dilated eyes upon me, "what are you talking about? What have I done? What do you mean? You must not go!"

And her hand sought mine and closed over it with an appealing, seducing touch. It went through my nerves and frame like flame. It seemed to confuse and scatter speech, sweep it from me as some useless trifle, and wake one intolerable burning desire for action.

I withdrew my hand suddenly, unbent my arm, and leaning

over the intervening chair side, put it round the low exquisite waist and tried to draw her towards me. But this most irritating of women resented immediately that which she had just invited.

"You must not!" she said, vehemently, trying with both hands to disengage her waist from my arm, her face changing uncertainly from white to scarlet, her eyes meeting mine with a fugitive alarm, which nearly, but not entirely, overwhelmed a furtive transitory look of pleasure at the contact.

I had not mistaken her, I thought, she was both weak and sensual. I must conquer the first quality, and seduce the second, and the battle was won. But it was hard to prevent my own self-command slipping from me, and if I did not keep that, my real object would be lost in this useless sort of coquetry, or possibly a quarrel. I wanted all my own judgment - and it was difficult to summon it and keep it - to tell me exactly how far to push matters to excite her, without driving her to get up and leave me altogether.

"Nonsense!" I said, looking down into the changing face and on to the heaving, panting bosom; "if we are engaged, you know, I have a right to do much more than put my arm round your waist."

"Right!" she repeated, scornfully, "there is no right except what I choose! Take your arm away!"

"Listen to me," I said quietly, paying no heed to her request, except to tighten my clasp just so much as I dared.

Such a waist it was, yielding, supple, and warm; it was maddening to have to restrain the muscles in my arm and regulate their pressure. The blood went to my brain, and it was with a severe effort I collected my thoughts.

"You say," I continued, "that I must not go. Lucia, there is only one single condition on which I will stay."

"What is it?" she murmured.

She had ceased to resist my arm now. The colour was hot in her face, and her eyes confused.

"That you name some definite and definitive date for our marriage."

"This question again! How you do torture me! It worries me to have to think about it!"

"I know, dearest; that is why I say, settle something, and don't think about it any more."

"How can you be so absurd!" she answered, leaning her head back against the chair, and averting her soft, flushed face as far from me as she could, so successfully that there was little view of anything except the white throat and under-part of her chin as she strained her head back from me.

"Please let things go on as they are."

The words were a positive entreaty, but they fell upon ground where passion had blocked access to any of the tenderer, impersonal feelings. I only felt a rage of impatience as I heard her.

"No, dearest," I said very gently; "that is just what they cannot do;" and I looked at the swelling neck with the faint blue veins visible in its transparency, and thought, "You must be my own, or I must cease to see you, otherwise I shall strangle you."

"I cannot stand this sort of thing any longer. Not even for you, Lucia, can I run the risk of losing the little brains I possess, which is extremely likely to happen if I let things, as you say, go on as they are."

"Why?" she said, fretfully, turning her head from side to side. "What do I do to you?"

I did not answer this, but I raised myself so that I could look into her face, and our eyes met. She flushed crimson, and did not repeat the question.

"You will kill me if you worry me like this!" she said, evasively, and she did actually look very ill at the moment.

"My sweet, why do you not trust me with the cause of all this hesitation? Are you afraid of me, or do you misunderstand me? Lucia, the woman I have once loved is the woman I must always love. Whatever had happened, whatever she had done, whatever I had heard of her or from her, I should love her still. Has anything occurred since you were with me in Paris that you are afraid to tell me of? Has anyone else come between us? If so, tell me. I shall understand everything. If there is anything to forgive, I will forgive everything. I swear there is nothing that can make any difference to my love for you."

Lucia looked me steadily in the face now. A contemptuous smile curved her lips, all the confusion died out of her eyes, and they filled with a limitless arrogance and self-reliance. I had my answer in her face. It was the face of a woman whose virtue is absolutely invulnerable, and whose honour is unshadowed, and who has suffered too acutely in the maintenance of both to hear the faintest hint of weakness without a smile. A fierce, delighted satisfaction ran through me before she spoke.

"What do you insinuate, Victor?" she said, lightly, but with pointed directness. "That I have been in love with two men at the same time? No; nothing of my own will nor my own action stands between us. Forgive, forsooth!" and she gave a delightful, mocking laugh.

"You are the person to be forgiven, if anybody, for inflicting this year upon me! Now, I ask you to wait a little and you won't!"

"Because I don't see any adequate reason," I returned. "Last year I told you mine, now I demand yours."

I kept my arm round her, and could feel the pulses in her waist throb under it, but I turned my eyes away from her and stared fixedly at the carpet, waiting for her to speak, with the best patience I could command.

"I have told you till I am tired of telling you I must get better first," she said, pettishly.

"But you are not getting better," I persisted.

"On the contrary, all these four months you have been getting steadily worse."

So long a silence followed this that I looked into her face again suddenly, the lips were quivering, and the eyes brimming with tears. She turned her head away, but not before I had seen them.

"Dearest, would you rather I released you from your promise to me?" I said, bending nearer over her. "Do you wish that?"

One single, violent sob shook the lovely breast beneath me and swelled the throat.

"No," she said, passionately; "you know I don't!"

"There is no alternative between that or our marriage," I said, quietly.

I was not trying to be inflexible, nor to harden my heart against her. It was hardened by passion, which at no time is an inspirer of tenderness, and mine had been sufficiently irritated through four months of alternate excitation and resistance to be determined now. My difficulty was not to avoid being too tender, but to check myself from being too harsh. Had I heard my own words in cool blood they might have seemed hard, and my insistence inconsiderate and blamable, but my calm was only artificial, and my judgment little else than a blind clinging to the object with which I had come.

"Why can't you go away for a time and then we can marry later, when you come back?" she answered, in a weak, evasive tone.

"It is not wholly a question of being away from you," I returned. "So long as I am engaged to you, Lucia, my whole life is totally different from that which it would be if I were not."

"I give you permission to lead any life you please," she said vehemently.

"Thank you!" I thought, sarcastically; "but your permission has nothing to do with it."

"It is useless to discuss the matter," I said aloud. "I cannot argue the point with you; I have said there is no third alternative."

"I think you are most unkind," and Lucia let two lovely arms and hands sink over the sides of the chair in gesture of weak despair.

I noticed, indifferently, that she was unnaturally pale.

"If you consent to our marriage, Lucia," I urged, pressing that alluring waist, "I will promise this, if it will simplify matters - you shall continue to live as if you were unmarried until you yourself put things on another footing."

She glanced at me quickly, as I spoke, with an unexpressed surprise.

"Then what would you gain?" she said, coldly, and the unveiled cynicism in the words went home.

I flushed.

"The certainty," I answered, briefly. "This indefinite state of things is simply intolerable."

She was silent for a second; then she said violently, the scarlet flowing over her face up to her eyes -

"No! It would be impossible to maintain such relations as those after marriage, and you know it! That is quite out of the question!"

I merely shrugged my shoulders in silence.

"I am waiting for your answer, Lucia," I said, after a few moments.

"And if I cannot give you one?"

"Then I leave town to-morrow morning."

She gave a fleeting glance into my face, and then suddenly burst into a passion of convulsive sobs and tears - sobs that seemed to tear her breast asunder, and tears that started in a blinding torrent, drenching her eyelids and eyelashes and pale cheeks.

"It is most unkind, it is horrible, it is cruel of you to press me in this way!" she sobbed, trying with both hot, trembling hands to push my arm away and to free herself from my clasp.

The sight of her tears hurt me, the pain stamped on the soft face, and the tumultuous rising and falling of her breast in those agonised sobs, reproached me, but the hurt and the reproach were dull. If she thought her tears would induce me to hesitate or to desist, she was wrong. They were to me simply a favourable sign of her weakness, and urged me to press my advantage. I felt instinctively that it would not do to fail now; having gone so far, I must go farther, and be successful.

Probably I should be much sooner forgiven by Lucia herself. Nothing is less pardonable, either in love or war, than an unsuccessful attempt.

Her resistance was nothing but nervous folly and weakness, and I believed she herself would be glad to be forced to give it up. Besides, even if my reason had not told me all this, my own feelings would have been enough to make me relentless.

"You may cry," I thought, looking at her as she sobbed with her head strained away from me, "but before I go you shall speak."

"What is your decision?" I said.

"What am I to say?" she murmured, in a voice choked by tears.

"Promise me some fixed date."

"I can't - now - like this. I will tell you to-morrow."

"No; to-day. You have deferred it from week to week. You must tell me now."

Silence, broken only by the sound of tears.

I waited, determined not to lose my patience.

"Tell me," I repeated after a pause.

"Victor, you must lend me your handkerchief," she said, turning her streaming eyes towards me.

The tears rained down over her lips and chin, and fell on the silk collar round her neck. She could not take her own handkerchief from her pocket, sitting as she was with my arm round her. I drew out mine and dried the wet eyes, and then pressed the soft reluctant head against my shoulder. Once there, it remained, too weary to lift itself again.

"Tell me, dearest."

"What, Victor?"

"The date."

"What date?"

"The thirteenth of next month," I said, decidedly.

I felt a startled quiver shoot through her.

"Oh, I could not really settle it without - without - thinking."

"Yes, you can, and must."

"But I don't know how long that is."

"It is exactly three weeks from now."

"But why the thirteenth?"

"We must appoint some date, and that is when my book appears in Paris, that's all; but choose another, if you like."

"The thirteenth is unlucky."

"What do you gain by all this trifling, Lucia?"

Some slight accent of all the angry surge of feelings within me crept, perhaps, into my tone. She did not answer, but began to cry again, not passionately this time, but in a weak, enervated listlessness.

"You are most unkind, Victor!"

"Is it to be the thirteenth?"

"I never knew you to be like this before."

"May I count it as the thirteenth?"

Silence. I waited and glanced at the clock again. The whole morning had slipped away. I should infallibly be late for that luncheon, but I could not help it.

"Lucia!"

"What, Victor?"

"Is it the thirteenth?"

"I don't know."

"Then I tell you that it is."

Almost beside myself with irritation, and uncertain whether I most loved or detested her, I drew her violently round towards me, bent over her and pressed my lips on hers, wet, ice-cold, and quivering. If there is anything in magnetism, or power to subdue another's volition, it ought to have acted fully then. I myself was at that moment the incarnation of will. My whole system was bowed to the intense effort to make her, by force, say what I desired.

"Say yes," I insisted.

She struggled violently, and the lips fluttered dumbly under mine; her breast swelled against mine; her soft hand tried to push back my shoulder.

"Say it," and I pressed her lips harder.

Either the force of the stronger will, or mere passion - and I am inclined to think the latter - had its influence.

"Yes, then, yes," she said, in a faint convulsive murmur, that was only just audible, but with the whole accent of assent in it.

"You promise?"

"Yes, I promise, absolutely. Oh, let me go. I am suffocated."

I released her instantly. I had no desire to keep her now that the point was gained, and I did not believe from her character that once having spoken she would retract. She started up, rose from the chair apparently with difficulty, made a few steps as if to cross the room, staggered, and, before I could reach her, fell heavily her full length along the floor. Her head, with its soft mass of bright hair, struck the ground almost at my feet, the pale face, drenched with tears, turned upward to the light. God! what a brute I felt! What had I done? I felt as if I had struck her. The first impulse of tenderness towards her welled up over my passion and turned it to a desperate self-reproach. A second later, Mrs. Grant came into the room.

"What has happened?" she said quickly, and then, as her gaze took in Lucia's figure, she turned to me with a blaze of anger in her eyes. "What have you been saying?" she exclaimed. "I will not have these scenes, Victor! I shall forbid you to see her!"

She fell on her knees beside Lucia, and unfastened the collar of her dress, still wet and stained with tears.

"Shall I not lift her up?" I asked, and Mrs. Grant raised her face again to me, white with suppressed anger.

"No," she answered, curtly. "Will you kindly leave this room. Your presence here is not needed."

I looked towards the fallen figure on the rug. The light head and the stone-white face seemed to multiply into a thousand replicas, and eddy round me. I walked out of the room.

"It will never be," I thought over and over to myself as I went down the stairs.

I turned into the dining-room, and flung myself into an

armchair and waited there. Everything but Lucia herself was forgotten. My consciousness seemed suspended almost as completely as hers. At last the door opened, and Mrs. Grant herself came in. She started on seeing me.

"You still here, Victor," she said coldly.

"How could I go?" I murmured. "Is she better?"

"Yes; she is better."

Mrs. Grant's face was white and composed, her tones like ice. I saw she was unwilling to trust herself to speak to me even.

"May I not speak to her for one minute?"

"Certainly not. Are you not satisfied with the mischief you have done already?" Her voice shook with suppressed indignation. "She tells me she has fixed the thirteenth for your marriage. So that is the subject you came to press to-day! I think your conduct is most disgraceful."

My attitude of mind was - I don't care two d - s what you think. However, I merely said, -

"I think you do me an injustice. I did not mean to distress Lucia to-day; but what is the use of this sort of thing going on as it has been doing? I have offered to release her from the engagement if she wishes, and in that case, I should go away altogether. I don't see that to keep up our present relations is any benefit to either of us."

Mrs. Grant's eyebrows relaxed a little.

"Perhaps you are right, Victor," she said, with a sigh. "Only we must be careful, or we shall lose her altogether."

Her voice shook now with something that was not anger. I held out my hand.

"I will come in the evening," I said, gently, "to hear of her if I cannot see her. May I?"

Mrs. Grant smiled, we shook hands, and I went out. I walked absently up the pavement, and then stood looking out as absently for a hansom. Now I had pushed matters to the point, I had not delayed nor put off action in this case, and I had attained the object with which I had come, but somehow I did not feel so satisfied as I had anticipated I should when I came away victorious.

Things were so different now from what they had been a year ago, and as I stood there looking up and down for a crawler, above the noise of the London thoroughfare, her own words to me in Paris rang with terrible distinctness, that prophecy wrung from her in the agony of her woman's longing - "I shall never be your own."

I almost believed it now.

"Looks like it," I thought, as I hailed a coming crawler and got in.

I said nothing to the man, but I suppose he had noted my glance at my watch before I got into the cab, and, in the hopes of an over-fare, he began lashing his horse across the head and neck. It was this that roused me out of a gloomy reverie, and I pushed up the trap.

"If you touch that animal again I'll get out," I said, angrily, as the poor brute tossed his head from side to side.

"Beg pardin', sir! Thought you was in a 'urry, sir!" came through the roof.

"Drive decently, and don't think," I muttered, relapsing into my own thoughts, cutting as the lash on the chestnut's neck.

I had stopped the lash, but I could not stop my thoughts. After dinner that evening I went to see her again. In this I did not succeed. I was told she had already gone to bed, but she had left a message for me, and not a word was said about rescinding the promise that had been forced from her in the morning. On the whole I went away satisfied and relieved.

"She will be all right," I thought, "now she has once made up her mind. It is extraordinary; women seem to have as great an aversion to forming a decision as children have to taking medicine."

"What should I do with myself now?" I questioned, standing idly in the hot, dusty London street. It was too early for me to go to bed, and I knew the pater would have turned in before I got back. I sauntered down two streets, and then drove to the Club. In the card-room I found Dick and two other fellows, one of whom was a stranger to me. As I made the convenient fourth, we played a rubber at whist. After this it seemed generally voted that the weather was too fatiguing for the strain of whist, and an adjournment was made to an open window, chairs, and drinks. I was preoccupied with my own thoughts, and I sat listening fitfully to the other men's gossip. Sometimes a sentence came to me; at one moment I was listening without hearing, the next I was hearing without listening. At last the phrase struck me - "Yes; dying horribly, like a rat of phosphorus."

I looked across to the man sitting opposite me. He was a young fellow, and I had gathered from to-night's conversation that he was studying medicine.

"Who is that?" I asked, with a sort of idle curiosity.

"Oh, only a fellow in the hospital," he answered with a cigarette between his teeth. "A paying patient. D. T., you know. I saw him last night in the ward. Shan't see him there to-morrow night, I expect," he added with a laugh, bringing down his rocking, tiled chair on its four legs, and determining at last to light the cigarette.

"You wanted to see the death, I thought," remarked Dick.

"I did; but, hang it, the fellow's been dying so long, my curiosity's worn out. However, I may come in for the show to-morrow morning if I am down at the hospital in time."

There was rather a cold silence after this remark, which made the young fellow look up and then add, hastily. -

"He's such an awful coward, you know, one can't feel much sympathy for him. 'Oh, it's so hard to die,' he goes on, 'at twenty-three! Can nothing save me? It seems so hard at twenty-three!' Well, I suppose no one does like going out, but still if a fellow knows he's got to" -

He paused. No one spoke for the minute, and then he went on, -

"Brought it on himself, too; I never saw a fellow so thoroughly knocked out! And now he does nothing but whine over it - 'Oh, I'd do so differently if I had my time over again!' I said to him last night, 'Now, look here, Johnson, why don't you try and console yourself with thinking you enjoyed life at the time?'"

"Did you say Johnson?" I asked. "What is his Christian name?"

"Howard," he answered.

The two other men started, and looked at me. The speaker glanced at them, and then added hastily to me, -

"Do you know him?"

"Slightly," I answered, coldly.

He coloured.

"I am sorry if I" -

"Not at all," I said. "All that concerns him is quite a matter of indifference to me."

There was a pause, and then, by tacit mutual consent, the topic was not renewed. The men spoke of other things, and I sat in silence.

So Howard had killed himself - was dying in this way, like a poisoned rat. It was, as I had said, a matter of indifference to me. I did not feel one pulse of sorrow or regret. It is strange how completely and entirely these emotions of love, affection, friendship, hate expire, and leave no trace of their past existence.

I hear and read much of "lingering memories," "clinging remembrance," but for me the tender track of a past affection does not exist. He had, as I had told him, cut out our friendship by the roots, and I heard now of his approaching death as that of an absolute stranger.

I wondered idly where was that softening influence, and on what sort of natures did it act, that is supposed to survive all dead attachments, all broken friendships. Certainly, according to tradition, it seemed as if I ought now to feel some sort of emotion at hearing the fate of a man who had once held so large a share of my affections.

There ought to have been some touch of sentimental sadness in my thoughts, some recollections of first days together, and so on. But there was none. By that night's work he had made himself as nothing to me henceforward.

I wondered in a desultory way whether the sudden complete annihilation of an emotion in the human heart in this way showed the hardness of the heart, or the magnitude of the offence, or the poor quality of the emotion itself; and then I was roused by Dick's voice saying Good-night to the other fellows, and he and I were left by the window alone.

He looked across at me, and said. -

"If you would like to see Howard, I believe Thompson could get you admission any time."

His voice was low and sympathetic.

I raised my eyebrows and said, -

"What should I want to see him for?"

Dick looked surprised, and then said, hesitatingly, -

"Surely you were very great friends at one time!"

I laughed.

"Yes," I answered, "but there is a great deal in that at one time!"

A few days later my father pointed out the announcement of Howard's death in The Times as we sat at breakfast.

I nodded.

"Yes; I heard at the Club he was dying."

"What was it? They don't say here."

"No," I said; "they would not."

"What was it?"

"Excess."

We neither said anything further with reference to it, but Howard's death was in both our thoughts, and as we got up from the table he said, suddenly, -

"There's a great thing in having a quiet, moderate nature, or at least self-control," and then he added afterwards, as if struck by a sudden amending thought, "Well, of course, that comes virtually to the same thing."

"Does it?" I thought. "By Jove, not to the man himself!"

"Would you think, then," I asked, with a smile, looking across the rug at him as we stood by the fire, "that the existence of a lion-tamer was quite the same as that of a maiden lady who kept cats?"

He laid down his paper suddenly and stared at me.

"I don't understand - I - you don't mean that you" -

"I mean," I said, "that it's extremely difficult to see the best course. Howard has just died, raving mad, for giving way to his impulses; I may die, raving mad, for controlling mine."

He looked at me apprehensively. "I am sorry, Victor, if - You don't think you have overworked, do you?"

I laughed as I met his eyes scanning my face anxiously for traces of the possible insanity.

"No; none of the slates are loose at present," I said. "That's all right, but I am seedy altogether; out of sorts all round - that's all."

CHAPTER VII

One unbroken flood of golden sunlight lay like a fallen silken veil over the points and peaks of the downs, over the swelling sides and the soft rolling dip of the valley, and the still September blue stretched cloudless overhead. It was the late afternoon of the thirteenth, a day that had been hot, oppressive, stifling in town, but here was simply warm, still, and tranquil.

All through the early hours of the day a parallel - if one may use the idea - oppression to the heat in the stirless air had weighed upon me. We had been married that morning, and before the ceremony my one sensation had been that of strain, during it tense anxiety, and afterwards reproach, and none of these are pleasant emotions. When I looked back to the morning, now, it seemed to be in the far distance; I don't know why, but ages seemed to have elapsed in the hours of this day.

Lucia had come up to the altar, her face whiter, more absolutely colourless than the veil over it, and my heart sank with apprehension as I first caught sight of her. Never, except in death, and already with the coffin enclosing it, have I seen a face so pallid. She walked steadily - she was a woman who always walked well, as a swan swims well, by nature - and the graceful figure passed on calmly towards us.

She kept the lids drooped over her eyes, and her white lips were closed firmly in repose. It seemed like a statue moving, and for a second I felt as if the church, the people, she, I, the whole scene were unreal, and my own blood changing into stone. The next second she was beside me, and then she suddenly lifted her eyes.

They glowed upon me as if there were actual fire stirring in the lustrous black pupils, and they gave back the joyous beat to my pulses, and sent my blood flowing onward again. The glance made us both human directly. But how anxious I felt all the time. Would she faint? I asked myself, desperately, over and over again. The colour of her face was terrifying, and the hand she gave me for the ring was cold as the touch of snow, and trembled convulsively. How long it all seemed! and how I loathed the prayers and the hymns, and sickened at the address! What earthly good is it to match words against a man's passion? As it is, it is, and no admonitions will alter it. However, all was over at last, and we were in the vestry. Lucia could not write her name; she tried, for no woman had less affectation and more self-command than she had, but the tremulousness of the fingers would not be controlled, and the mere effort agitated her so that she fell back in the chair, quivering, till each point of lace in her dress shook, and every eye could see the violent heart-beats under her bodice.

"Don't sign it, dearest!" I exclaimed, feeling like a murderer as I looked into the blanched, nervous face, and widely-dilated eyes.

There was a blank pause for a moment of sympathy and apprehension, as her shaking hand dropped the pen, and then the clergyman picked it up and finished the half-written name. I felt a sharp self- reproach, and Dick did not mend matters as he turned from her to me and said, in an indignant mutter, -

"She is not in a fit state to be married at all, Victor!"

He looked at me as if I were committing a crime, and I coloured and felt like a brute. Then there was the long breakfast, and the reception, and, as I say, it seemed as if centuries were rolling over my head in each five minutes, but now it was all done with; the burden of other's society had slipped from us, and the weight of my own oppression I seemed to have left, together with the sullen heat of town air. In all the journey down Lucia had been recovering. The scarlet had been coming back to her lips, and as the first breath of air came to us, straight from the heart of the smiling, sun-lit valley, they parted in a laugh, the light leapt up in the soft azure eyes, the rose-colour under the skin, and she bent forward to me and said, impulsively, -

"Victor, if you want to know, I feel perfectly happy!"

"And I, too, you darling!" I said, smiling back into the brilliant face.

"It seems quite a new thing to feel. I don't ever remember feeling happy until now, and I am five-and-twenty. Think, a whole third of an ordinary lifetime passed before I have known it!"

I laughed.

"Well, you are going to begin now, at any-rate," I said.

"Yes; I think so," she answered, both the carmine lips still curved in smiles. "But still it is late to begin. It is not wise; one should begin at fifteen - ten years back."

"Begin what?" I said, laughing.

"To be happy."

"By all means," I answered. "Begin as soon as you get the chance; but I think most people do. Only it is the chance that is generally wanting!"

"I don't know," Lucia said, looking away from me through the window, where the flying sunny slopes of the valley sped by.

"People muddle away their chances of happiness in life. Ten years ago, when I was fifteen and you were twenty - well, we might have married then, and felt all that we feel now a whole ten years ago, which I have passed without a single happy day."

A shade of sadness came into the eyes, and darkened them as she spoke.

"But why do you think of that now?" I asked. "It is no use. The ten years have gone beyond recall, and, if you have not been happy, you have something to show for the time. You have been working."

"Yes," Lucia repeated; "I have been working."

There was silence. I hoped I had recalled to her thoughts the great canvas that stood complete in her studio. For myself, I knew that the keenest touch of pleasure that stirred my frame now was held in the ever-present thought that this day saw the birth of my work in Paris. Not for worlds would I have hinted this to Lucia. To have breathed a word that assigned even a part of my pleasure at the moment to anything but the possession of herself was the last thing that I would have done.

Every pleasure is kin to every other, and they each tend to enhance and strengthen another, so that in reality this inner pleasure of my thoughts that reverted constantly to the Paris publishers was no enemy, not even a rival, but rather a coadjutor of the passionate, personal pleasure in the woman beside me. The brain already intoxicated with one pleasant emotion lends itself more, not less, readily to another, just as a brutal lover inflames his love with wine. In precisely the same way, my passion for Lucia was inflamed by the wine of gratified ambition. All the same, I said nothing touching on the book for fear lest she should misunderstand me, nor hinted - that which I felt myself - that this scene put back ten years, when I was full of vague ambitions and unaccomplished plans, would not have possessed the zest it had for me now.

Man, unfortunately, is not the desirer of one thing at a time, but of many things, and the gratification of a single desire is not enough to content him. If a person is both hungry and thirsty, you cannot satisfy him, however kindly you may supply him with bread. Another line of thought that ran side by side with this in my brain, as I watched the shadow pass over the girl's face as she thought of her ten lost years, was, that had we had these sensations at fifteen and twenty they would certainly not have out-lasted us till now! But this also I would not say. The passing of our passions, however we may recognise it as philosophers, is not pleasant to us as lovers.

"Oh! there is our house, I believe!" said Lucia, suddenly, as we neared the station.

"Yes; you can just see it from the line, I know," I answered, looking through the window. "What a glorious evening!"

All before our eyes lay in the still, liquid golden light, and through the burnished haze that seemed to slope obliquely between us and it we saw the square white house, lying a little blow the level of the line, and all but hidden behind a delicate, intricate profusion of light green foliage. Behind it rose a rolling slope, clothed half-way up with a copse of young larch trees, whose slender stems sent long shadows down the whole length of its side, falling across the sun-baked, waving, brown-and-yellow grasses, and the red cows, lying lower down the slope, drowsy, as all else seemed in the mellow sunlight.

At the side of the house stretched a lawn, shaded-in from the carriage drive by a fringe of larch and spruce, and on this lawn, innocent of tennis-courts and similar abominations, were planted here and there single trees. It had been the fancy of the owner that not one of these on the lawn should be indigenous, and almost every country out of Europe was represented by one lovely forest denizen.

The crytomera, the cedar of Japan, raised its delicate rosy crest here under the blue of an English sky; a young Turkish cypress shot like a dart from the ground and threw its narrow shadow straight as a spear across the emerald turf; and farther on a small squat tree, from China, unfurled smooth, glossy, polished leaves of lightest green, and thick-lipped succulent scarlet flowers, indolently to the kiss of the British sun. We caught a passing glimpse of it, and Lucia drew in her breath softly, with pleasure.

"How lovely! What a pretty house, Victor!" she said.

"Yes; I know it is supposed to be a very charming place."

"And don't you think so, too?" she asked, turning to me, and the side light from the window caught the curly hair under the velvet hat brim and turned it into gold.

"I haven't got a very keen artistic eye, Lucia, I think. Certainly not for houses," I answered, laughing, and looking straight into those eyes of lapis lazuli and then away. "But I adore this one, as it is going to give me the happiest hours in my life!"

And I met her eyes. A slow flush mounted into Lucia's face, and then she seemed to tear her gaze from mine with difficulty and turned to the window, so that I could not see her face; her ear, however, betrayed her all the same, for the painful blush reached even there, and flooded its white, pink-tinted porcelain with scarlet.

A second after, the train was at a standstill, drawn up at the platform of the station. It was very quiet, and even the train coming in hardly seemed to disturb the sleepy stillness that hung over the strips of asphalt, the beds of hollyhocks and lilac bushes against the whitewashed walls, where the rural fancy of the stationmaster had gone so far as to range a row of straw bee-hives.

There were few passengers by the train, and little luggage except our own. The single porter, the stationmaster, some workmen, and a few market women, with white aprons and baskets of eggs on their arms, stared wonderingly at Lucia as she stood with the golden sunlight pouring down upon her light hair and brilliant face, and the glory of Parisian fashion embodied in her dress.

My friend's carriage had come to meet the train, and I left her for a moment to speak to the footman about our luggage. As I walked back up the platform she was standing three-quarter ways towards me, the attitude which displays best that most alluring line in a woman's figure, the line from under the arms to the waist.

In Lucia it was specially striking, not straight, but like the back of a Z, a sharp, smooth slope to the low waist, and formed a perfect harmony with the two curves of the hips, and the long fall of the skirt beneath. All my frame - every limb and muscle - quickened with keen pleasure as my eye met the familiar lines, as yet familiar to one sense only, and then followed the inevitable, involuntary rush of exultant remembrance of my absolute possession now.

I let it come and flood my brain with a half-drunken satisfaction, and the phrase formed itself on my lips, "Well, hang it, my to-morrow has come at last!" As I came up to her I saw her eyes were fixed upon me with a searching gaze. I thanked heaven Lucia was not one of the horrible, modern women, if indeed they exist outside a lady's novel, who are always analysing you and your emotions, and testing the depth of your inferiority to themselves. I believed she was only studying and weighing my outer appearance, of which I was far more confident than of the inner personality. So I met the blue, soft-shaded eyes in the flare of the sunlight without embarrassment, and smiled back into them as I joined her.

"Well, darling, now come," I said; "I think I have made that idiot understand your hand-bag is not to be shaken!"

Lucia pushed a little pale gloved hand through my arm, impetuously, and said, as we turned to follow the decline of the platform towards the carriage, -

"Victor! you are so good-looking!"

I laughed. I was right, then. She had only been thinking of the exterior. What a comfort! A few steps had brought us to the carriage door, and the servant was holding it open. I waited to answer her till we had started, but when she had got in, and I had followed, she threw herself back on the cushions and put one hand on my shoulder, and before I could speak she went on in a low voice, -

"Yes! It is very charming now, of course; but all the same you have nearly killed me!"

The words were spoken with such a bitter, tremulous vehemence, that I turned and looked at her in startled silence. Her eyes still passed keenly backwards and forwards over my face.

"Oh, yes! if you knew one-tenth of what I have suffered this last year! how I have coveted - longed. It doesn't matter what I say to you now, does it! Oh, I am so glad that all this terrible repression and restraint is done away with, and that we are free to do and say what we like! I am so glad I am your wife at last!"

The trembling, excited accents, springing straight from her thoughts, and poured into my ear from her warm, parting lips, stirred my own tolerably well-governed feelings to a painful intensity, and I felt only too sharply that I, at any rate, had not done with self-restraint. I said nothing. I was rendered dumb by the riot within me, but I pushed my arm round her waist and drew her against me.

The violence and want of tenderness in the action pleased her, perhaps, being a woman. The waist yielded gladly, and the whole form sank against me with relaxed and satisfied pleasure.

We neither of us spoke again until the carriage drew up

between the bright green of the larches, stabbed through with long shafts of light, and before the shallow steps and open windows of the house. On each side of the steps stood, not classic urns to remind one irresistibly of graveyards, but honest, bright, terracotta, human-looking flower-pots, from which rose or trailed the loveliest plants a skilful gardener could wrest from September. A white peacock paced majestically across the red gravel towards the larches, and underneath these, swinging exuberantly on suspended perches, with the strips and bars of sunlight flashing on their glittering feathers, chattered together nearly a dozen Oriental parrots.

Lucia looked at the scene with an artist's quick eye, and I heard an instinctive murmur about its making a pretty sketch.

I told her she would be otherwise occupied now than in making sketches, and we both laughed as we passed up the steps together.

In the hall hovered, like two evil shadows, her maid and my valet, lying in wait for us to remind us of clothes and the serious duties of life. I saw Lucia carried off from me with despairing eyes, knowing it would be ages before I saw her again.

It did not take me long to get into another suit, and then I returned to the dining-room, and roamed about from end to end, too restless to sit down to glance at the papers that lay on the different tables, or even to light up a cigar. I walked about aimlessly, longing for the woman's presence beside me again.

It was a very large room - two, properly, knocked into one - with a window looking to the front and the carriage-drive, and another at the side, opening, with French glass doors, on to the low stone terrace which overlooked the lawn.

Through these I wandered at last on to the terrace, and rested my arms on the low balustrade, looking with unseeing eyes across the lawn, with its tropical trees standing motionless in the golden haze. Everything around me was very still, and a peculiar strained calm seemed to be upon me also - the calm of an intense desire, hushed and expectant, in all the blood.

A swift, hurried step came on to the terrace, and I turned instantly.

The light fell all over her, the living incarnation of my long drawn out hopes and dreams. She had changed her dress to a light dinner-silk. The bodice was modest - I mean by that, it was unobtrusive - very. Excess of nervous excitement, the wealth of evening sunlight, and her fashion of dressing made her dazzling to look upon, and I stood for a second in silence.

She misunderstood my pause and glance, and a rush of hot colour came into her face, and the tears suddenly started to her eyes.

"You don't like my dress," she exclaimed. "I told Celine she was cutting it too low!"

A step forward and I had her in my arms. Ah! what were dreams to the keen, sharp delight of feeling her there - alive, and in the flesh - throbbing and pulsating against me? I declared the dress was perfect, that I would not have the bodice half an inch higher for anything, that she looked adorable, and so on, until she was comforted. The tears passed into laughter, and the flush died away; but she trembled against me distressingly, and her lips quivered nervously.

I held her to me, but she seemed to flutter uncertainly in my clasp, just as a bird flutters wildly without aim at the limit of its tethering cord, and when I released her she sank into the wire chair at our side with a look of exhaustion stamped on the soft, delicate face. I saw that it would require all my tact and care to make this evening a success, and I determined that it should be one for her. Standing there beside her, looking down on her light head, I made a rough, mental examination of my thoughts. I seized those that had anything of self in them, rolled them hastily together, and thrust them into an obscure corner of my brain out of hearing, to leave the better part of my love for her free to guide me.

I drew a chair close to her and sat down, letting my arm rest along the top rail of hers, behind the soft head, which, after a minute, sank gently back upon it with a movement of tired relief. We neither spoke, and the perfect, sunny calm of the evening air, the silence, and the physical rest seemed to soothe her. When the servant came on to the terrace to announce the dinner, she had recovered, and her arm on mine was warm and firm.

As soon as we had finished dinner, she rose restlessly from the table and looked at me with a hesitating air. I smiled back at her, but it hurt me inwardly this want of confidence, this lack of familiarity she seemed to have. This sort of hesitation before she made the simplest request, the start and flush when I spoke suddenly to her, this timidity of me now, hurt and puzzled me. I, who had taught my dog implicit trust, seemed to have missed the way with the woman.

I remembered Paris: my own harshness to her there came back upon me like a blow. The indelible impression of my hardness had been given then, and she dreaded it now. She had been conquered then; her will and desire had been broken down to mine; she had been forced to yield and to suffer; she had appealed to me and found me inflexible, relentless; and now I had the fruits of my victory. The woman I loved, though she might love me, feared me instinctively, as the once well-beaten dog ever afterwards fears its master.

To me, who hated victory, who loathed subduing others, and the price they bring of fear and shrinking, the realisation of her feeling towards me was like a sudden physical pain. I got up from the table feeling my face grow white with sharp distress. I hardly knew at the moment how to express my thoughts; besides, I knew words would be of no avail. An impression given is a scar upon the mind like a scar upon the flesh. She fixed her eyes on my face with a sort of apprehension in them, that was extremely bitter to me.

"What were you going to say, dearest?" I said, merely, with a faint smile; "go on."

"Oh, nothing much!" she said, hastily, flushing and paling almost in the same moment; "only I feel so restless. Come and show me all the rest of the house, will you?"

I assented, and we passed out of the dining-room into the hall and up the shallow flight of stairs. I put my right hand on the banister and my left arm round her waist, and the whole sweet figure beside me, and the white neck and ear so near me, drove out the thoughts of a minute back, and I only laughed as I felt her waist contract convulsively as I touched it.

"Would you like to take my arm better?" I said, mockingly, and drew her round to me so that the soft face was just beneath my own. In the subdued light of the staircase she lifted her lids, and I saw her eyes, gleaming and sparkling, brimming over with gaiety and pleasure, and the arm next me she raised and twisted close round my neck.

"No, Victor; here is the place for my arm now! You won't push it away as you did in Paris, will you?"

The words hurt cruelly. Could I never obliterate that wretched memory? It was vivid with her; it clung to me. It seemed a shadow dogging my present pleasure. I stopped suddenly on the staircase and took her wholly into my arms. All the supple form yielded at my touch, till it leaned hard against my own; the face, pallid with excitement, was raised to mine; the glitter of her eyes swam before my vision as I caught it from beneath the half-drooped lids; the lips, parted in a faint breath, then closed as mine joined them. As they touched, no consciousness was left except that both our lives seemed mingling, panting, fainting on our lips.

The pain that is pleasure, and the pleasure that is pain, thrilled and pierced every nerve as I held her and felt those lips under mine, her heart beat under my heart, her weak arms twisted round my throat. When at last my lips set hers free, on fire with the passion of my own, they moved in a half-delirious murmur, -

"Victor, you don't know how I love you!"

I have no distinct recollection of passing up the remaining stairs, but we did reach the landing, and a second or two later were standing in the drawing-room. I think she said it was pretty, and so on, but I hardly heard, my head was reeling, and all my senses dull, her figure leant a little against me, and the pressure of her arm was upon mine. After the drawing-room, the reading-room, and a breakfast-room, all opening from the same corridor, had been passed through, there were still two rooms unexplored on that floor. I turned the handle of the nearer door, and then pushed it open.

Lucia stepped on to the threshold, and then I felt her arm start violently in mine, and she drew back with a sharp, instinctive movement.

I looked down upon her and murmured, -

"Our room, dearest."

The colour blazed all over the fair skin, till it seemed scorching it, and tears startled into the dismayed eyes, which she turned from me confusedly, as she shrank back into the passage.

I was startled, and a chill seemed to fall upon me, and penetrate deeper as a grey pallor succeeded to the burning flush, and she had to lay one trembling hand on my arm again for actual support.

"Victor, it is nothing!" she said, hurriedly, forcing a smile to her lips.

"It - it - startled me."

She made a nervous step forward, as if she would have forced herself to enter the room with me, but I collected myself with a great effort, and gently drew the door shut.

"There is another sitting-room a little farther on; come and look at it," I said, quietly, in a light, indifferent tone, as if we were meeting in society for the first time.

I drew her on past the door, feeling her hand fluttering on my arm, and her feet uncertain beside my own. Inwardly I was alarmed - dismayed. Her extreme nervousness, and the physical effect upon her, frightened me. With crushing force and clearness came back to me the remembrance of the fearless, eager, unrestrained abandonment of body and mind, the gay exuberance of careless passion, with all the vigour of youth and health in it, that had leapt up to meet my caress a year ago, - and been refused. We passed on to a door on the other side of the corridor, which opened to another sitting-room. A lovely evening had given way to a lovelier night. Beyond the long window panes, set open to the still air, we caught sight of the sinking golden crescent of the moon towards the south; above and all round, to the low horizon, the sky was crowded, sparkling, and brilliant with stars. I moved two chairs close up to the open window, but she stood by the sill and leaned forward to the night air.

"You think me very silly?" she said, with her head turned away from me.

"I think you are not well, dearest," I said, gently.

There was silence. Words seemed frozen on my lips. A sort of terror filled me of exciting or embarrassing her. I stood beside the window frame watching her. After a minute or two she dropped back into a chair and looked up at me with a laugh.

"I think I am all right, only you startled me! By the way,

Victor, if anything ever does happen to me, you will remember you have your work and your talent to turn to, won't you? I mean you would not do anything desperate. I want you to promise me that."

She lay back in the easy chair, burying her light head and polished white shoulder in the velvet cushion, and swinging one little foot idly as she looked up smiling for her answer. The bright light in the room fell full upon her, and I looked down upon this brilliant piece of life, full of glowing tints and warm pulses and subtle powers, and my brain flamed with the pleasure of the senses. I hardly noted her words.

"Dear little girl!" I said, smiling back into her eyes. "I refuse to think of such things at all!"

"Oh, well, it doesn't matter! I don't expect you would," she said, laughing, the colour leaping up in her cheeks, and the vivid blue deepening behind her lashes. "Come and make much of me now while you have got me."

Her whole face and form were instinct with a delicious invitation, and I bent down to and over her, filled with the delight of the moment. We made one chair do for both of us, and looked through the window at intervals to escape each other's eyes, and laughed at nothing, and talked a very extraordinary astronomy. At last, with her soft fingers in my hair and on my throat, and her white arm above the elbow clasped in my hand, speech, even laughter, grew choked in dense feelings for all the command I kept upon myself; and we sat in silence, hearing each other's breath, feeling each pulse that beat in the other's throat and breast.

There had been a long silence when the last star of Orion slid over the horizon, followed by my impatient eyes. I looked at my watch. I hardly know why I did it then. It was an involuntary action rather than a conscious one. I did not say anything as I replaced it, but she glanced sharply at me, and I saw her lips whitened.

I knew the intense excitement that was moving her, it spoke to me in every line of her form - in her eyes, torn wide open by it, in the faint gleam of sweat that showed on the white forehead. I was not blind to it, but the tumult within me, made all the greater by the sight of it, left me insensible to its danger for her.

She got up from where we were sitting, and began to walk restlessly round the table. I wheeled my chair slightly round so that I could watch her. Nothing struck me particularly as I did so except the extreme grace and attraction in the moving form. The heavy silk skirt dragged backwards and forwards over the carpet almost soundless, the moonlight and gaslight alternately gleaming on its folds. Each time that she came between me and the table my eyes followed with dizzy delight the soft side curve of her breast, the lines of the exquisite waist, the white idle hand that sometimes touched the edge of my chair arm, sometimes not, as she passed. One of these times I caught it and detained her, and looked up at her face, but the light was behind her, and only fell on the bright hair.

"Why do you walk about so?" I asked.

"I don't know. Victor, I feel very strange. I hope nothing is going to happen. I never felt quite like this before;" and she broke her hand loose from me and passed on.

I sprang up and followed her, and put my arm round her.

"Going to happen, dearest! What do you mean? Do you feel ill?"

I looked at her. She was very white, and her lips were parted and pale. There was a distressed and strangely absent look upon her face which startled me, though I had no clue to its significance.

"Yes, very ill," she answered, her eyes wandering away from my anxious ones looking down at her, as we stood for a moment together.

Then she gently pushed away my arm and continued her walk.

"You know my heart always does beat and hurt if I am very happy, or very excited, or any thing, but it's never been quite so bad as this before." And then, catching the distress upon my face, she added, "I daresay this is nothing. It will go off. I think it is only hysterical. Don't look so unhappy!" And a faint smile swept over her pallid face.

She made her way to the sideboard and drank some water standing there. Then she continued to move slowly round the room, both hands pressed beneath her left breast, and her delicate eyebrows contracted into one dark line across her colourless face.

"I overworked myself so tremendously just lately," she said, after a minute, "after - well, after I came to you in Paris. I shall take a long rest now. I hope I shall get strong again. When one is as delicate as this, life is not worth having."

And then, before I could answer, she stopped suddenly, and looked across the room at me with dilated eyes.

"Is there any brandy I could have?" she asked, abruptly.

My handbag stood in the corner of the room. There was a flask of brandy there. In two seconds I had got it out and was beside her with the traveling-glass half filled.

She took it with a fluttering, uncertain hand, and drank a little, but not even then did the colour come back to her lips - they were apart and grey. She set the glass down on the table with a wandering, undecided movement, and then turned towards me and linked two ice-cold hands round my neck, -

"Hold me up! I am sinking!" and her head fell heavily against my shoulder.

I clasped my arm firmly round her waist. I was startled, distressed, alarmed, but still, even then, I did not think there was any serious danger. I thought she was hysterical, as she had said; over-strained, and over-excited. I thought at most this was a fainting attack. I thought - God knows what I thought. I must have been blind.

She put her hand to her throat, and I saw she wanted air. Supporting her, I crossed to the window, and stood where the cool night breeze came blowing in upon her face. My hand followed hers to her bodice, and I loosened all the delicate lace ruffles round it that it had never been my privilege to touch till now, and that were no whiter than the lovely breast from which I unloosed them.

So we stood for a few seconds, her lids were drooped over her eyes. At intervals, it seemed to me, her heart gave great single, convulsive throbs that thudded through both our beings.

Then suddenly she tore her eyes wide open, and fixed them in an unreasoning agony upon me. A straining, fearful effort seemed in them. I pressed her to me.

"What is it, dearest?" I said quietly, trying to recall her to herself. "Why do you look at me so?"

"Because I cannot see you! I have lost my sight! Oh, Victor, I am DYING!"

The words were a strained cry of terrified anguish, and they cleft through my brain like the stroke of an axe. With blinding suddenness I knew then what was coming. My heart seemed turned into stone. Only Reason rejected the truth. The gong stood on the table close beside us. I stretched out my arm and struck it furiously, my eyes fixed in terror on her face. The Great Change was there; the shadow already of dissolution. The door was thrust open and a servant hurried in.

"A doctor!" I said to him, "quick for your life."

But I saw, before any doctor could reach us, she would have gone from me. I strained my arms round her.

"Speak to me, my darling, speak," I said wildly, raising the dying head higher on my breast.

Both her hands were clasped hard upon her heart. A frightful agony was reflected in the bloodless face, but for the moment death retreated.

"Victor! To think I am dying! I shall never paint again! Oh, don't let me go! Keep me! oh, keep me with you!"

My brain seemed bursting as I heard her. The only prayer of my life broke then in a frenzy from my lips, "Great God! spare her!"

"Hold me up! oh, keep me, Victor! I am dying."

"Dearest, you are fainting!"

There was no answer. Heavier and heavier the pressure grew on my breast, the arm slid heavily from my shoulders, the head fell slowly backwards on my arm. I looked into her eyes. They were black as I had seen them long ago in the studio. Fearfully, terribly dilated they were, and in their depths was that look as if the soul were listening to a far-off summons, calling, calling to it, to depart.

"My life! Speak to me once more! One word!"

Probably my voice did not reach her. For her already the silence held but that one imperious command. My brief rule of this spirit was over. It no longer heeded me. She no longer answered me. Her eyes were still fixed upon me in helpless horror, terror, and despair; but they knew me no longer. The unwilling soul had already started on its journey, and its earthly love was no more to it than its earthly form. I held her motionless, my eyes on hers, then I saw a glaze, a slow glaze fit upon them, they set in it, and it told me she was dead.

Without a struggle, without a spasm, without a deeper breath to mark the severance, her soul had drifted away from me, out of her body that I held in my arms. Without a farewell, without a word, without any knowledge of the second when the life had fled, without a sound beyond that despairing, terrified appeal to me to keep her. I stood rigid, petrified, my arms locked round her like iron bands. I heard the door open and steps. Then I saw the doctor before me. He gave one glance at the drooping head.

"Lay her down flat," he said.

I lifted her into my arms wholly, and walked through the door into the corridor to the opposite room - our room, and laid her on the bed. He followed me to the bedside and bent over her. I drew back and stood beside the curtain motionless. Everything was swaying before my eyes in darkened confusion. Was this my wedding night? There was the room, full of warm, shaded light; there was the bed, and on it a passive woman's figure, and another man bent over it and tore aside the bodice and unclasped the white stays.

I watched his hand part them and pass indifferently beneath them, and beneath the linen, and rest over the left breast and then beneath it. The shade grew colder on his face. There was an intense silence in the room, then the words came across it, "Quite extinct." My ears seemed to fill with sounds, the ground to rise upward, the bed to heave, and I went forward blindly and tore his hand from her breast and pushed him from the bed.

"Then go and leave us," I said, and I heard my own voice as from a great distance.

He looked at me, and his face and everything around was dark before my eyes.

"Will you kindly go out of this room?" I repeated, and he walked to the door.

I opened it, he passed out, and I shut and locked it, and came back to the bed. The weight of nerveless, passive beauty on it had crushed a depression in its whiteness, the head had sunk down sideways to the pillow as in tired sleep. Across the throat and breast, over and amongst the disturbed laces of her dress, and on the parted gleaming satin of her stays fell a flood of rose-coloured light. One shoulder rose from it and caught a shadow; another shade lay lower in the dimples of the elbow; the inside of the arm looked warm. The throat, the round soft throat, seemed glowing; the fallen head, the passive arms, the whole outstretched form seemed relaxed in the abandonment of sleep. Had I often seen her in my dreams like this? This was but the realisation of my dreams. I bent over her, then threw myself wildly upon the bed beside her, and drew her into my arms.

"Lucia! my Lucia!" The sweet face almost seemed to smile as I drew the head to me, and a soft curl of hair fell upon my arm as I pushed it round her neck and pressed her breast to mine. It came softly and unresistingly, just so much as my arm pressed it, with terrible compliance. The throat chilled through my arm to the bone, numbed it.

I laid my other hand upon her neck, pushed it lower till it rested above her heart, and enclosed one breast, nerveless, pulseless, and cold, colder than any snow. Slowly it chilled through my fingers. I smoothed one passive arm - how cold. Then my hand sought her waist, and my arm leant upon her hip - as once in Paris - and here the coldness held and froze me.

Through her silk skirt it penetrated; the damp, eternal coldness pierced through my quivering, living arm; it seemed dividing my veins like steel.

It was a dead woman that I clasped: a corpse. I strained my

eyes down upon her face, that seemed but asleep.

"Lucia?"

And the word was one frenzied, senseless question; and the sweet mouth seemed to smile back, in its last eternal smile, my answer, -

"Yes, I am Lucia, and you possess me now."

Like a torrent dammed up for a moment, the flood of insensate, impotent desire flowed again, raging through all my veins, and engulfed me; my burning arms interlaced her, my weight pressed upon her, my trembling lips, full of torturing flame, sought hers, met, closed upon them in a frenzy of vain, fruitless longing and stayed - frozen there.

When I was hardly well from weeks of raving illness that followed, but yet well enough to walk and go about like a rational being, I went to the cemetery to see all that now remained to me beyond my own fearful memory. Dick was beside me. He had insisted on coming with me, and, when we reached the grave, he stood beside me at its edge, as he had stood beside me at the altar.

A huge slab of white marble lay horizontal upon the narrow, single grave. Fools! They should have made it a double one. A heavy iron chain, swinging great balls, studded with spikes, was linked from post to post round the tomb. At its head rose a cross, extending its arms against a background of cypresses.

I looked at it all with dry and savage eyes. The illimitable regret, the boundless, hopeless remorse for the irrevocable that has been shaped by our own heedless hands, the unspeakable yearning for that, once more, which has been freely ours and we have flung away, rose like a swelling tide within me, and rolled through me in thundering, deadening waves standing at her grave. I stared half blindly at the words on the stone - "Wife of V. Hilton." Wife! What a mockery!

I looked, and that slab of white marble - spotless and relentless - that barred her into the grave, seemed to my still half-unstable brain symbolical of that last year of virgin purity of life that had broken her strength to bear. That spiked iron linked round the helpless dust seemed like the chains of repression that had tortured and crushed the soft ardent nature. That arrogant cross, stretching its arms threateningly above the lonely tomb, seemed the cross upon which we had crucified - she and I - the desires of the flesh. And at its foot, I read, - "She sleeps to waken to a glad to-morrow." And then a bitter laugh burst from my lips.

"Who put that?" I asked. "Great God! that that word should follow me even here!"

Dick took my arm.

"We know nothing. There may be a to-morrow;" at which I merely laughed again.

"Wife of V. Hilton!" I repeated, reading from the stone. "If she had been, Dick, it would not have been so hard."

Dick said nothing. After a time he urged me to come away from the grave.

"Where? To what?" I asked him; and we both stood silent, gazing upon her cross.

. . . .

Months have passed by, and Dick consoles me still, and tells me I shall refind the zest of life by and by, later on, in the future, to-morrow.

Choose from Thousands of 1stWorldLibrary Classics By

A. M. Barnard
Ada Leverson
Adolphus William Ward
Aesop
Agatha Christie
Alexander Aaronsohn
Alexander Kielland
Alexandre Dumas
Alfred Gatty
Alfred Ollivant
Alice Duer Miller
Alice Turner Curtis
Alice Dunbar
Ambrose Bierce
Amelia E. Barr
Amory H. Bradford
Andrew Lang
Andrew McFarland Davis
Andy Adams
Anna Sewell
Annie Besant
Annie Hamilton Donnell
Annie Payson Call
Annonaymous
Anton Chekhov
Arnold Bennett
Arthur Conan Doyle
Arthur M. Winfield
Arthur Ransome
Atticus
B.H. Baden-Powell
B. M. Bower
Baroness Emmuska Orczy
Baroness Orczy
Basil King
Bayard Taylor
Ben Macomber
Bertha Muzzy Bower
Bjornstjerne Bjornson
Booth Tarkington
Boyd Cable
Bram Stoker
C. Collodi
C. E. Orr
C. M. Ingleby
Carolyn Wells
Catherine Parr Traill
Charles A. Eastman
Charles Dickens

Charles Dudley Warner
Charles Farrar Browne
Charles Ives
Charles Kingsley
Charles Klein
Charles Amory Beach
Charles Hanson Towne
Charles Lathrop Pack
Charles Whibley
Charles Willing Beale
Charlotte M. Braeme
Charlotte M. Yonge
Charlotte Perkins Stetson
Clair W. Hayes
Clarence Day Jr.
Clarence E. Mulford
Clemence Housman
Confucius
Cornelis DeWitt Wilcox
Cyril Burleigh
D. H. Lawrence
Daniel Defoe
David Garnett
Dinah Craik
Don Carlos Janes
Donald Keyhoe
Dorothy Kilner
Dougan Clark
Douglas Fairbanks
E. Nesbit
E.P.Roe
E. Phillips Oppenheim
Earl Barnes
Edgar Rice Burroughs
Edith Van Dyne
Edith Wharton
Edward J. O'Biren
Edward S. Ellis
Edwin L. Arnold
Eleanor Atkins
Eliot Gregory
Elizabeth Gaskell
Elizabeth McCracken
Elizabeth Von Arnim
Ellem Key
Emerson Hough
Emilie F. Carlen
Emily Dickinson
Enid Bagnold

Enilor Macartney Lane
Erasmus W. Jones
Ernie Howard Pie
Ethel Turner
Ethel Watts Mumford
Eugenie Foa
Eugene Wood
Eustace Hale Ball
Evelyn Everett-green
Everard Cotes
F. H. Cheley
F. J. Cross
Federick Austin Ogg
Ferdinand Ossendowski
Francis Bacon
Francis Darwin
Frances Hodgson Burnett
Frances Parkinson Keyes
Frank Gee Patchin
Frank Harris
Frank Jewett Mather
Frank L. Packard
Frank V. Webster
Frederic Stewart Isham
Frederick Trevor Hill
Frederick Winslow Taylor
Friedrich Kerst
Friedrich Nietzsche
Fyodor Dostoyevsky
G.A. Henty
G.K. Chesterton
Gabrielle E. Jackson
Garrett P. Serviss
Gaston Leroux
George A. Warren
George Ade
Geroge Bernard Shaw
George Durston
George Ebers
George Eliot
George Gissing
George MacDonald
George Meredith
George Orwell
George Sylvester Viereck
George Tucker
George W. Cable
George Wharton James
Gertrude Atherton

Grace E. King
Grace Gallatin
Grant Allen
Guillermo A. Sherwell
Gulielma Zollinger
Gustav Flaubert
H. A. Cody
H. B. Irving
H.C. Bailey
H. G. Wells
H. H. Munro
H. Irving Hancock
H. Rider Haggard
H. W. C. Davis
Hamilton Wright Mabie
Hans Christian Andersen
Harold Avery
Harold McGrath
Harriet Beecher Stowe
Harry Houidini
Helent Hunt Jackson
Helen Nicolay
Hendrik Conscience
Hendy David Thoreau
Henri Barbusse
Henrik Ibsen
Henry Adams
Henry Ford
Henry Frost
Henry James
Henry Jones Ford
Henry Seton Merriman
Henry W Longfellow
Herbert A. Giles
Herbert N. Casson
Herman Hesse
Homer
Honore De Balzac
Horace Walpole
Horatio Alger Jr.
Howard Pyle
Howard R. Garis
Hugh Lofting
Hugh Walpole
Humphry Ward
Ian Maclaren
Inez Haynes Gillmore
Irving Bacheller
Israel Abrahams
Ivan Turgenev
J.G.Austin

J. Henri Fabre
J. M. Barrie
J. Macdonald Oxley
J. S. Fletcher
J. S. Knowles
J. Storer Clouston
Jack London
Jacob Abbott
James Allen
James Andrews
James Baldwin
James DeMille
James Joyce
James Lane Allen
James Lane Allen
James Oliver Curwood
James Oppenheim
James Otis
James R. Driscoll
Jane Austen
Janet Aldridge
Jens Peter Jacobsen
Jerome K. Jerome
John Burroughs
John Cournos
John F. Kennedy
John Gay
John Glasworthy
John Habberton
John Joy Bell
John Kendrick Bangs
John Milton
John Philip Sousa
Jonas Lauritz Idemil Lie
Jonathan Swift
Joseph A. Altsheler
Joseph Carey
Joseph Conrad
Joseph E. Badger Jr
Joseph Hergesheimer
Joseph Jacobs
Jules Vernes
Julian Hawthrone
Julie A Lippmann
Justin Huntly McCarthy
Kakuzo Okakura
Kenneth Grahame
Kenneth McGaffey
Kate Langley Bosher
Kate Langley Bosher
Katherine Cecil Thurston

Katherine Stokes
L. A. Abbot
L. T. Meade
L. Frank Baum
Latta Griswold
Laura Lee Hope
Laurence Housman
Lawrence Beasley
Leo Tolstoy
Leonid Andreyev
Lewis Carroll
Lewis Sperry Chafer
Lilian Bell
Lloyd Osbourne
Louis Hughes
Louis Tracy
Louisa May Alcott
Lucy Fitch Perkins
Lucy Maud Montgomery
Lydia Miller Middleton
Lyndon Orr
M. Corvus
M. H. Adams
Margaret E. Sangster
Margaret Vandercook
Margret Penrose
Maria Edgeworth
Maria Thompson Daviess
Mariano Azuela
Marion Polk Angellotti
Mark Overton
Mark Twain
Mary Austin
Mary Catherine Crowley
Mary Cole
Mary Hastings Bradley
Mary Roberts Rinehart
Mary Rowlandson
M. Wollstonecraft Shelley
Maud Lindsay
Max Beerbohm
Myra Kelly
Nathaniel Hawthrone
Nicolo Machiavelli
O. F. Walton
Oscar Wilde
Owen Johnson
P.G. Wodehouse
Paul and Mabel Thorne
Paul G. Tomlinson
Paul Severing

Percy Brebner
Peter B. Kyne
Plato
R. Derby Holmes
R. L. Stevenson
R. S. Ball
Rabindranath Tagore
Rahul Alvares
Ralph Bonehill
Ralph Henry Barbour
Ralph Victor
Ralph Waldo Emmerson
Rene Descartes
Rex Beach
Rex E. Beach
Richard Harding Davis
Richard Jefferies
Richard Le Gallienne
Robert Barr
Robert Frost
Robert Gordon Anderson
Robert L. Drake
Robert Lansing
Robert Lynd
Robert Michael Ballantyne
Robert W. Chambers
Rosa Nouchette Carey
Rudyard Kipling
Samuel B. Allison

Samuel Hopkins Adams
Sarah Bernhardt
Sarah C. Hallowell
Selma Lagerlof
Sherwood Anderson
Sigmund Freud
Standish O'Grady
Stanley Weyman
Stella Benson
Stephen Crane
Stewart Edward White
Stijn Streuvels
Swami Abhedananda
Swami Parmananda
T. S. Ackland
T. S. Arthur
The Princess Der Ling
Thomas A. Janvier
Thomas A Kempis
Thomas Anderton
Thomas Bailey Aldrich
Thomas Bulfinch
Thomas De Quincey
Thomas H. Huxley
Thomas Hardy
Thomas More
Thornton W. Burgess
U. S. Grant
Valentine Williams

Various Authors
Vaughan Kester
Victor Appleton
Virginia Woolf
Walter Camp
Walter Scott
Washington Irving
Wilbur Lawton
Wilkie Collins
Willa Cather
Willard F. Baker
William Dean Howells
William le Queux
W. Makepeace Thackeray
William W. Walter
Winston Churchill
Yei Theodora Ozaki
Yogi Ramacharaka
Young E. Allison
Zane Grey